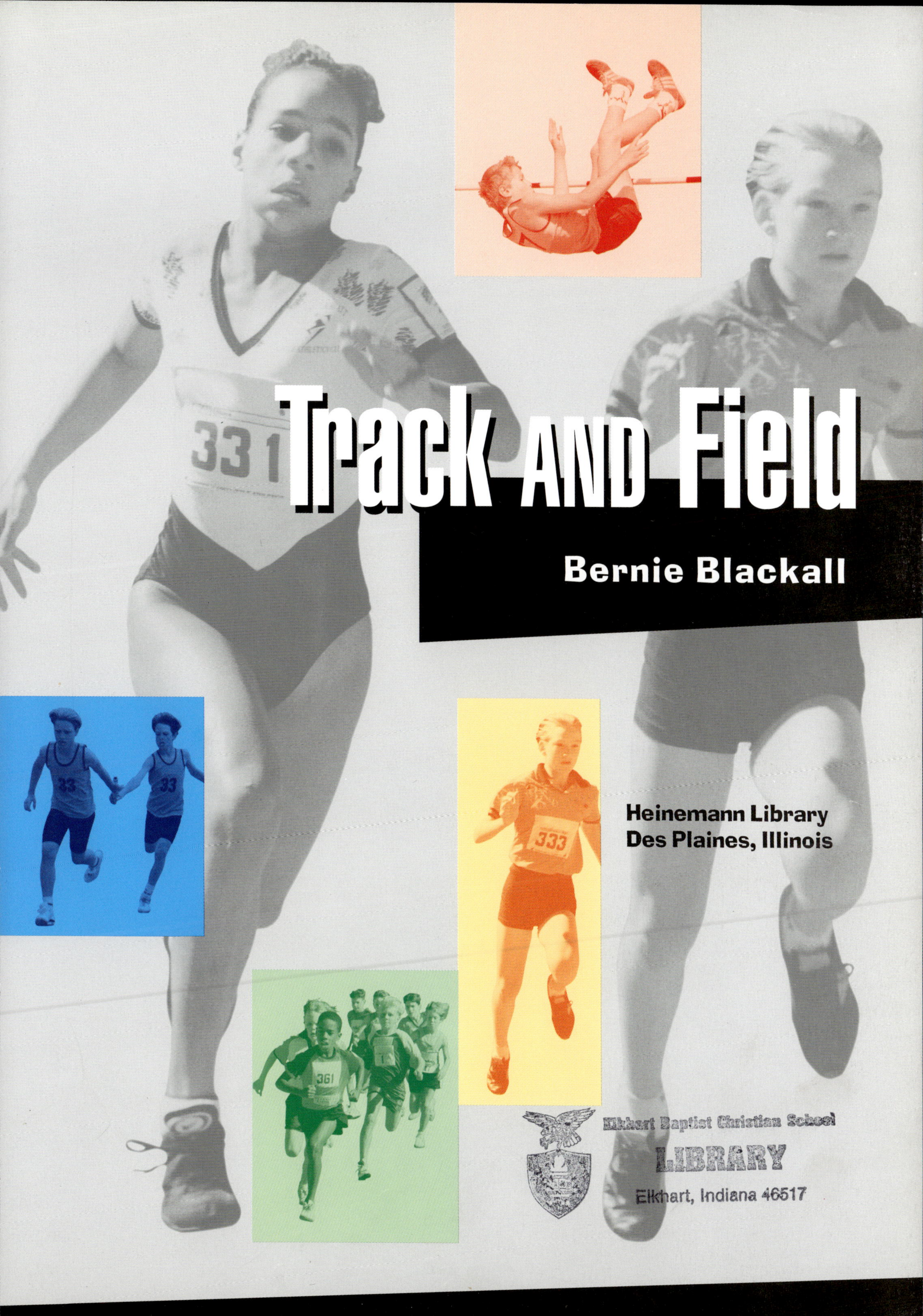

Track and Field

Bernie Blackall

Heinemann Library
Des Plaines, Illinois

© 1999 Reed Educational & Professional Publishing
Published by Heinemann Library,
an imprint of Reed Educational & Professional Publishing,
1350 East Touhy Avenue, Suite 240 West
Des Plaines, IL 60018

All rights reserved. No part of this publication may be reproduced or transmitted in any form or by any means, electronic or mechanical, including photocopying, recording, taping, or any information storage and retrieval system, without permission in writing from the publisher.

© Bernie Blackall 1999

03 02 01 00 99
10 9 8 7 6 5 4 3 2 1

Series cover and text design by Karen Young
Cover by Smarty-pants Design
Paged by Jo Pritchard
Edited by Jane Pearson
Illustrations by Xiangyi Mo and Jingwen Wang
Production by Alexandra Tannock
Printed in Hong Kong by Wing King Tong

Library of Congress Catalogng-in-Publication Data
Blackall, Bernie, 1956
    Track and Field/Bernie Blackall.
       p.   cm -- (Top Sport)
Includes bibliographical references (p.) and index.
Summary: Introduces track and field, discussing its history, U.S. highlights, individual track and field events, and skills.
    ISBN 157572843 5   (lib. bdg.)
    1. Track and Field - Juvenile literature. [Track and Field.] I. Title.
    II. Series: Blackall, Bernie, 1956-- Top Sport.
796.42

Acknowledgements
The author and publisher are grateful to the following for permission
to reproduce copyright material:
Ancient Art & Architecture Museum, pp. 8, 9; Duomo/Stephen E. Sutton, p 6;
The Little Athletics Association of Australia, pp. 4, 5, 13, 14, 17, 19, 22, 25, 27;
Malcolm Cross, p. 10; Sport /The Library, p. 15; Wies Fajzullin, pp. 11, 16;
Liles Photography, pp. 21, 24; Allsport/Gary Mortimore, p. 7.

Every effort has been made to contact copyright holders of any material reproduced in this book. Any omissions will be rectified in subsequent printings if notice is given to the publisher.

Some words are shown in bold, **like this**. You can find out what they mean by looking in the glossary.

Track and Field requires specialist instruction. Do not attempt any of the sports without a qualified, registered instructor present.

Special thanks to Coach Michael "Hoot" Gibson of Lake Mary's Girls' Track, Lake Mary, Florida, for his assistance in the preparation of this book.

Contents

About Track and Field   5
U.S. Highlights   6
History of Track and Field   8
The Track
    Sprints   10
    Relays   12
    Hurdles   14
    Distance Running   16
    Race Walking   17
The Field
    Javelin   18
    Discus   20
    Shot Put   22
    Long Jump and Triple Jump   24
    High Jump   26
Getting Ready   28
Taking it Further   30
More Books to Read   30
Glossary   31
Index   32

About Track and Field

There are several sports or events that make up track and field. These include running, walking, throwing, and jumping. Track events are races. The races are held on a track that surrounds a field. Field events involve throwing and jumping. Most of these events are held on the field inside the track.

Today's track and field events originated from ancient sports. They are a major part of the Summer Olympic Games where athletes try to run fastest, throw farthest, and jump highest or longest.

Track events
Sprints:
   100 m, 200 m, 400 m
Middle distance:
   800 m and 1500 m
Long distance:
   5,000 m and 10,000 m
Hurdles:
   100 m (women), 110 m (men),
   400 m (men and women)
Race walks:
   10 km (women),
   20 km (men), 50 km (men)
Relays:
   4 x 100 m, 4 x 400 m
Marathon:
   42.195 km
Steeplechase:
   3,000 m (men)

Field events
Throwing events:
   Javelin
   Discus
   Shot put
   Hammer
Jumping events:
   Long jump
   High jump
   Triple jump
   Pole vault

Tracks are usually eight lanes wide and 400 meters long. They usually have a synthetic weatherproof surface. Inside the track is the grass field.

Safety first
To participate safely, you will need to listen carefully to your coaches and the officials. It is important to observe the rules of safety to avoid injuring yourself or others.

Track and Field 5

U.S. Highlights

Michael Johnson

The first modern track and field events were held at the first modern Olympic Games in 1896 in Athens, Greece. There, an American named Thomas Burke won the men's 400 m run in 54.2 seconds. One hundred years later, another American, Michael Johnson won that same event in 43.49 seconds. He set a new Olympic record.

In the 100 years between 1896 and 1996, a whole wealth of Americans have stood on the top step of the ceremony platform, bowing to receive their Gold, Silver, and Bronze medals. Among them are other speedsters, such as Jesse Owens, Bob Hayes, Jim Hines; the jumpers like Carl Lewis, and super-athletes like decathlete Bruce Jenner.

Marianne Jones

Women didn't officially begin to compete in Olympic events until 1928. It was an American, Elizabeth Robinson, who won the 100 m race and the Gold medal in a record time of 12.2 seconds. In 1996, Gail Devers won that same race in 10.94 seconds. The record for that race, however, is 10.54 seconds. It was set in 1988 by Florence Griffith-Joyner. Griffith-Joyner's time broke the 28-year-old record held by Wilma Ruldoph.

In the relays, where the races are team competitions, the U.S. men's and women's teams have won 13 out of 16 races in each of the last four Olympic games.

Look for these stars on the track and in the field at the Olympic Games 2000 in Sydney, Australia:

Men: Michael Johnson, Joe Green, C.J. Hunter, Alan Johnson, Charles Austin, John Drummond, Eric Walder, John Godina, Bob Kennedy, Karl Lewis, John Davis, Charles Austin, and Maurice Green

Women: Marianne Jones, Sheila Hudson, Jackie Joyner-Kersey, Susie Hamilton, Rena Jacobs, Sara Miles Clark, Joetta Clark, and Connie Price Smith

Track and Field 7

History of Track and Field

Track and Field is one of the oldest sports. Competitions can be traced back more than 3,000 years to races run in Greece. Ancient art from many cultures is often decorated with scenes of races, throwing events such as **javelin** and **discus**, and jumping. It is believed that early humans used these skills for survival and hunting.

a medal from the ancient Olympic Games

The Ancient Olympics

Track was part of the ancient Olympic Games held at Olympia in Greece. The first recorded Olympic champion was Coroelous, a cook from Elis, Greece. He won the sprint race in 776 B.C. At that time, the Olympics was that single event. Sprinters ran the length of the stadium—about 211 meters. Over time, longer races and field events, such as javelin, discus, and long jump were added. Track and field competition was part of the games until the last ancient Olympics in A.D. 303. By then, they had lasted over 1,000 years!

The marathon

The **marathon** is named after a Greek legend. When the Greeks defeated the Persians at the Battle of Marathon, Pheidippides, a messenger carrying the news, ran 25 miles (41.83 kilometers) to Athens. He collapsed and died shortly after.

At the first modern Olympic Games, athletes raced over the same course that Pheidippides had run. The event became known as the marathon. At the London Olympics in 1908, the distance of the marathon was lengthened by 365 meters. This was done so that the British king could watch the end of the race from the comfort of his seat in the stadium.

This Greek urn, decorated with racers, is from the fourth century B.C.

The Modern Olympics

Some of the first "modern" track and field competitions were part of military training. In 1896, French Baron Pierre du Coubertin, revived the Olympic Games in Athens, Greece. Today the Olympics is the most important international track and field competition. It is the dream of many young athletes to compete in the Olympic Games.

Women were excluded from the ancient Olympic Games, both as competitors and as spectators.

Shot put

The shot put is a test of strength. It grew out of the ancient sport of stone throwing. In the British military, some soldiers began to use cannon balls, or "shots," instead of stones in their own competitions. The shot put, using a standard metal shot, was included in the Olympics at the first modern Olympic Games in 1896.

Track and Field 9

The Track
Sprints

Sprints are the shortest and fastest races. Outdoors, they are run over distances of 100, 200, and 400 meters. Indoors, 50-, 55-, and 60-meter sprints are run. Sprinters run the entire distance as fast as they can. Each runner must stay in his or her own lane.

The sprint start

Every fraction of a second counts in a sprint. It is crucial to get off to a fast start. There are two ways to start a sprint. The standing start is used by young children. Older athletes use the crouch start. **Starting blocks** are usually used for crouch starts because they help sprinters get the maximum push and acceleration. The blocks are placed at two foot lengths behind the starting line.

From the crouch start, move quickly and smoothly into the run.

The starter calls three commands: "On your marks," "Set," "Go."

On your marks

With your hands behind the starting line and palms up, make a bridge with your fingers and thumbs. Put your feet on the blocks so your weight is on the balls of your feet. Be sure your front knee is level with your elbows.

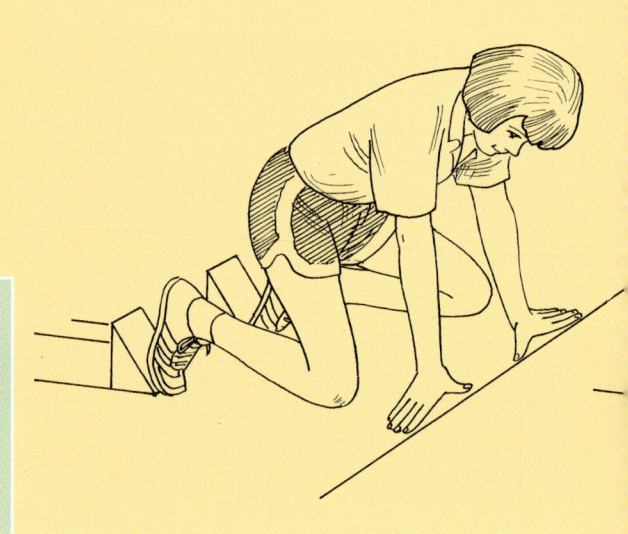

10 Top Sport

Running shoes

It is important to wear a good pair of shoes. The shoes support your feet as you run. Professional athletes and those in training, wear lightweight shoes with metal spikes called cleats, for extra traction.

The running action

In addition to getting off to a powerful start, it is important to move quickly into a strong run.

Hold your head steady and set your eyes on a point ahead of you. Keep your body relaxed as you lift your knees high. This helps you lengthen your stride. Lean your body forward slightly. Keep your elbows bent at about a 90 degree angle. Pumping your arms back and forth as you run will help you keep your balance.

the running action

Set

Raise your hips above your shoulders, keeping your eyes down. With your arms holding your weight, press your feet firmly against the blocks to get a strong push forward.

Go

Push off smoothly. Keep your head and body low. Pump your arms back and forth.

Track and Field 11

The Track

Relays

Relays are run by teams of four. A **baton** is passed from one runner to the next as quickly as possible. Each runner has a starting point on the track. The first runner from each team starts the race carrying the baton. He or she then passes it to the next runner at the **changeover zone.** The runner carrying the baton is called the incoming runner. The runner receiving the baton is the outgoing runner. There are two relay race distances: 4 x 100 m and 4 x 400 m. In the 4 x 100 m, all runners must stay in their own lanes. In the 4 x 400 m, they can move to the shorter inner lane after the first 500 meters.

Positions for a 4 x 100 meters relay race

As the incoming runner reaches the **acceleration zone** he or she shouts "Go." Both runners speed up. The baton is passed at top speed. On entering the changeover zone, the incoming runner calls "stick" or "hand" to ensure a smooth pass.

Staggered starts and changeover zones ensure that all teams complete the same distance on the curved track.

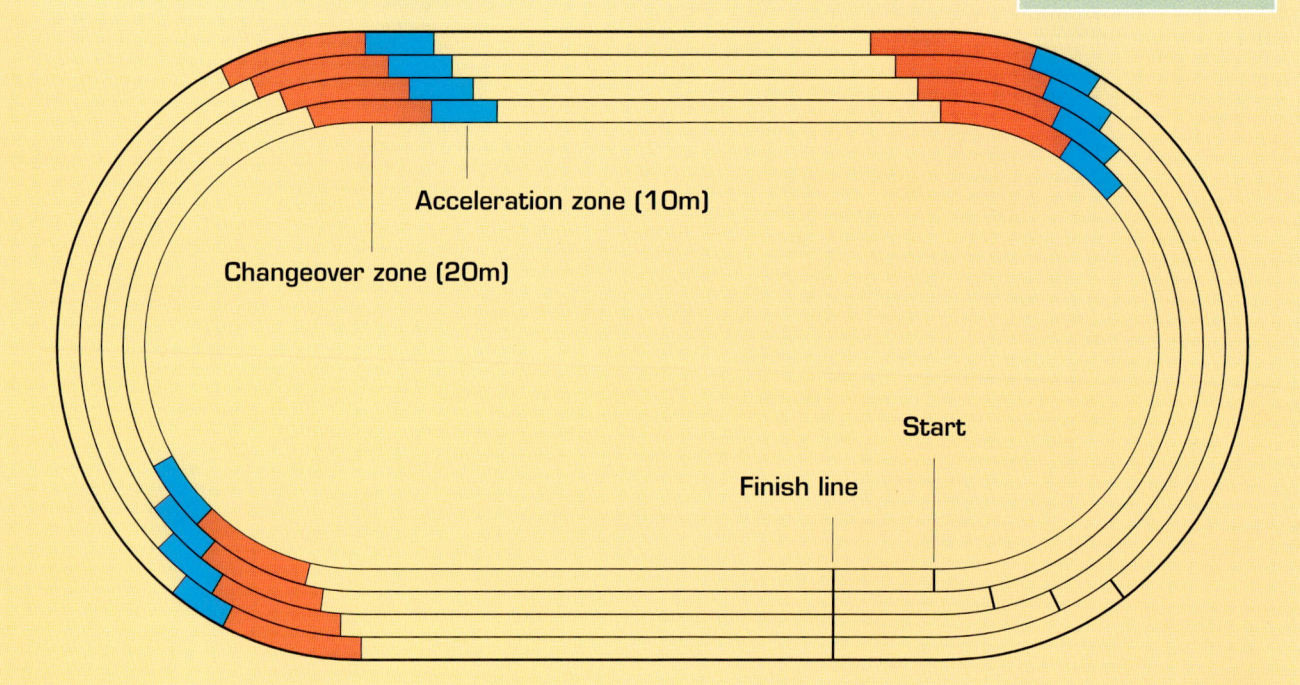

Acceleration zone (10m)

Changeover zone (20m)

Start

Finish line

12 Top Sport

Passing the baton

As the incoming runner approaches, the receiver speeds up and prepares to take the baton. If the incoming runner is carrying the baton in the right hand, the receiver reaches back with his or her left hand. The palm should face up and the thumb and fingers should form a V. The incoming runner passes the baton down into the hand of the receiver. The new incoming runner will sprint his or her leg of the race. The baton must be held in the hand in which it was received. The baton is passed alternatively from the right hand of one runner to the left hand of the next.

It is important not to look back as you receive the baton. That would cause you to slow down.

Practice your baton changes slowly at first. Then, when you have mastered the technique, add speed for a fast, smooth changeover.

The changeover

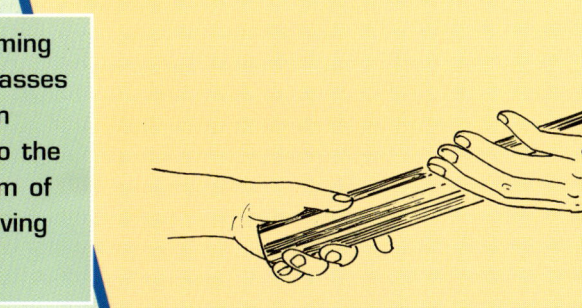

The incoming runner passes the baton down into the open palm of the receiving runner.

Track and Field 13

The Track
Hurdles

Hurdles is a sprint race in which the runners clear obstacles, called hurdles. It is important to move smoothly over the hurdles in a way that slows you down as little as possible. Keep low and avoid high jumps over the hurdles. That could cost you precious seconds.

If you take an odd number of strides between hurdles, you'll lead with the same leg each time. If you take an even number of strides, you'll lead with alternate legs.

The hurdle action

Establish a rhythm by figuring out how many steps to take between hurdles.

As you approach the hurdle, push yourself forward with your arms and off the ground with your trail leg. Straighten your lead leg.

Lean forward as you approach the hurdle. Use the arm opposite your lead leg to drive yourself forward.

The dip finish

Your finish is especially important because finishes can be very close. You have crossed the finish line when your body, not your leading foot, passes the line. If you "dip" your body just as you approach the finish line, you might just get the edge to win.

Debbie Flintoff-King dips to win the 400 m hurdles in Seoul

If you accidentally knock a hurdle, you will not be disqualified. However, knocking a hurdle will throw you off balance and slow you down.

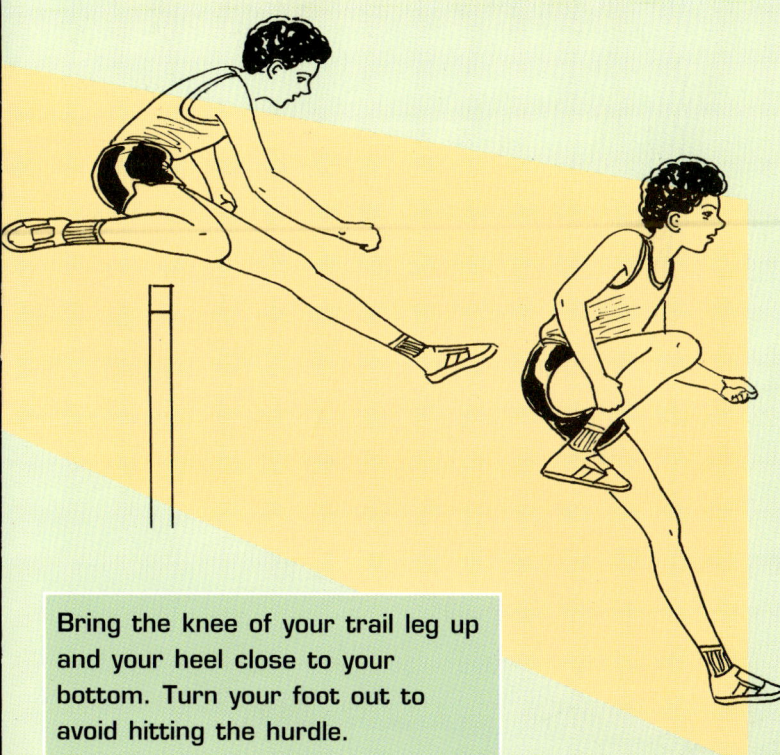

Bring the knee of your trail leg up and your heel close to your bottom. Turn your foot out to avoid hitting the hurdle.

Get your lead leg back on the track as fast as you can to regain speed. Land on the ball of your foot.

Track and Field 15

The Track
Distance Running

Middle and long distance running events require great stamina. The style of running and the rules for these events are different from those of the **sprints.**

The starter's calls for distance events are "On your marks" and "Go"—there is no "Set." The starting line is curved and runners don't use **starting blocks.** Competitors don't stay in individual lanes, but move across to the inside of the track soon after the start.

The distance running technique is geared for endurance, with an upright body position and less arm and leg movements than those used for sprinting.

Once the race starts, runners move to the inside of the track, since this is the shortest distance to the finish.

They move quickly to pass other racers, but are careful not to bump into or trip other runners. Runners try to keep up with the leaders, but pace themselves so that as other runners drop back, they have enough energy left to push themselves ahead.

Always be prepared to sprint across the finish line. Run your hardest across the line—put all you have into the last steps.

16 Top Sport

The Track
Race Walking

Walking is a track and field event. Competitors have a special way of walking so they move faster and take longer strides. They must follow certain rules to make walking fast different from running. A walker must always have at least one foot on the ground. The back foot must not leave the ground until the front one returns to it. The leg straightens as the foot touches the ground.

Keep your body upright. Use your arms to move you forward. Bend your arms and swing them across your chest to neck height.

Rotate your hips slightly before your foot lands to lengthen your stride. Place each foot down heel first and straighten your knee just as your foot hits the ground.

The Field Javelin

The **Javelin** is a throwing event. The javelin itself is a spearlike object. It is about 8 feet (2.5 meters) long. Competitors throw it as far as possible. The point does not have to stick in the ground, but it must land first.

The grip

There are two basic grips for throwing the javelin: for each one, place your hand towards the back of the grip area and keep your palm upwards. Try each grip to see which one is the most comfortable for you.

The throw

As a beginner, start by throwing from a standing position. When you have mastered that, add a few steps for a run-up. Then slowly build up speed to add force to your throw.

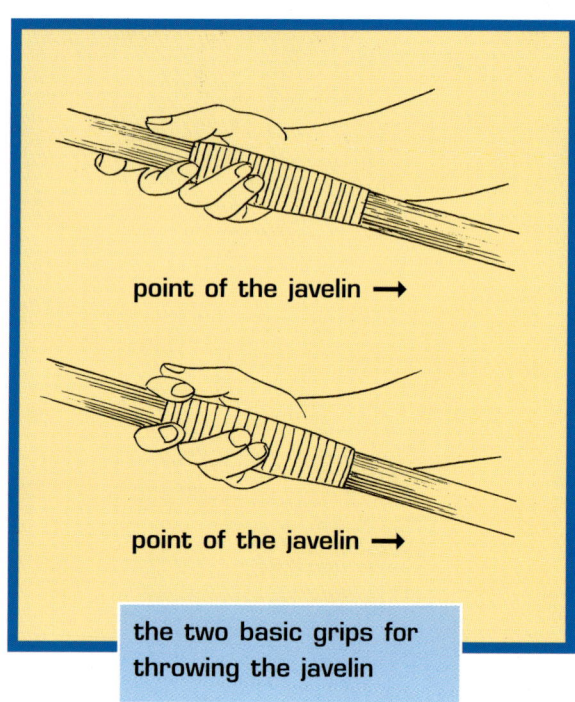

point of the javelin →

point of the javelin →

the two basic grips for throwing the javelin

Safety

It is very important to follow safety rules when competing in or practicing javelin throwing. Stand well clear of anyone throwing a javelin. Never throw a javelin if anyone is in or near the throwing area.

Start your run-up with the javelin at ear level, parallel to the ground.

Raise your arm and take the javelin back as you begin to turn side on.

18 Top Sport

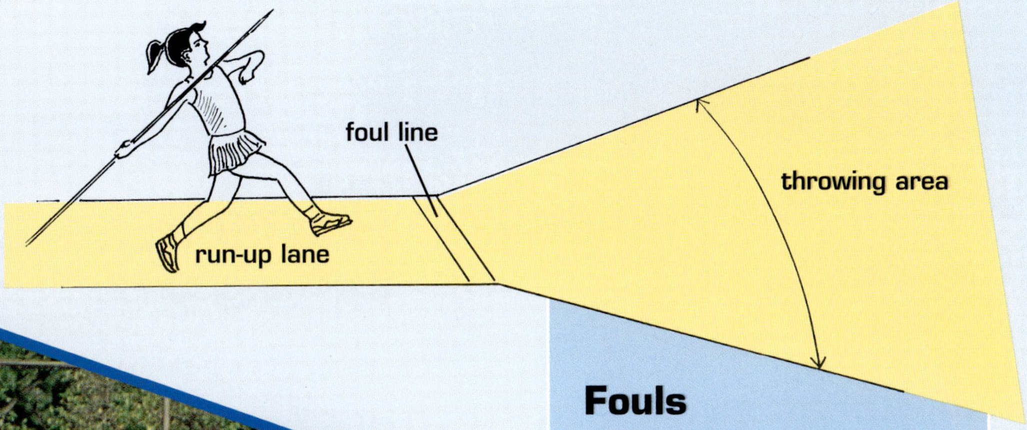

foul line

throwing area

run-up lane

Fouls

A foul is called when:
- the thrower steps over the foul line
- the javelin lands outside the throwing area
- the thrower crosses the foul line before the throw is marked
- the thrower fails to exit the runway from behind the foul line

As you release the javelin, your weight should be on the foot opposite your throwing arm.

Lift your other elbow high and take a long stride.

Drive the javelin forwards, leading with your elbow. Push your other arm back and around.

Flick the javelin with your fingers as you release it. Be careful not to step over the foul line.

Track and Field 19

The Field
Discus

The **discus** is shaped like a plate. Competitors throw the discus as far as they can. They throw from a metal-rimmed concrete circle into the **throwing area**. A swinging release sends the discus sailing. The thrower must stay in the **throwing circle** until the follow through. Competitors must enter and leave from the back half of the throwing circle. Usually each competitor has three throws and the best one is recorded.

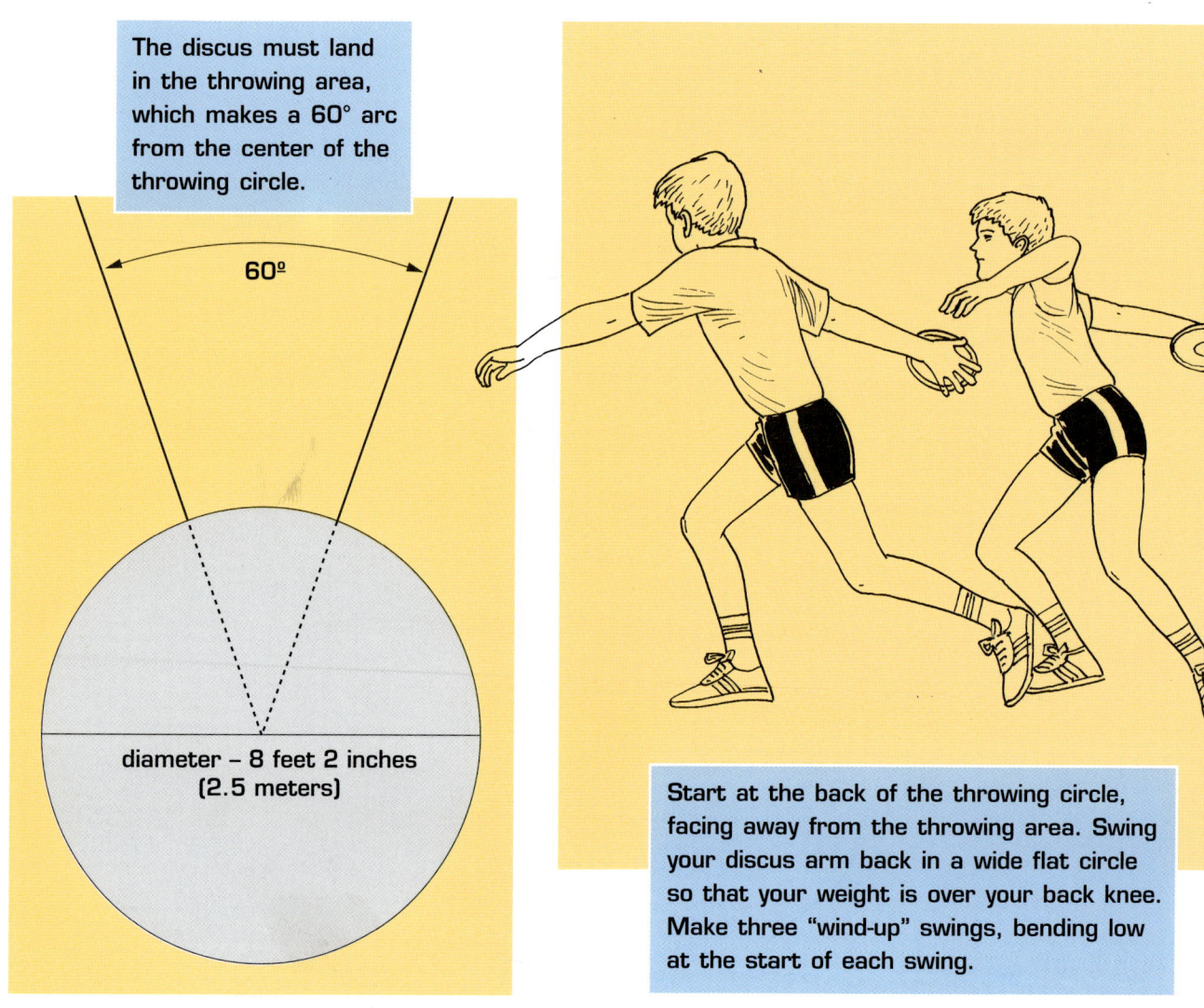

The discus must land in the throwing area, which makes a 60° arc from the center of the throwing circle.

60°

diameter – 8 feet 2 inches (2.5 meters)

Start at the back of the throwing circle, facing away from the throwing area. Swing your discus arm back in a wide flat circle so that your weight is over your back knee. Make three "wind-up" swings, bending low at the start of each swing.

The grip

Hold the discus flat against your palm and wrist. Spread your fingers so that they reach just over the rim. Your thumb should rest across the top for balance.

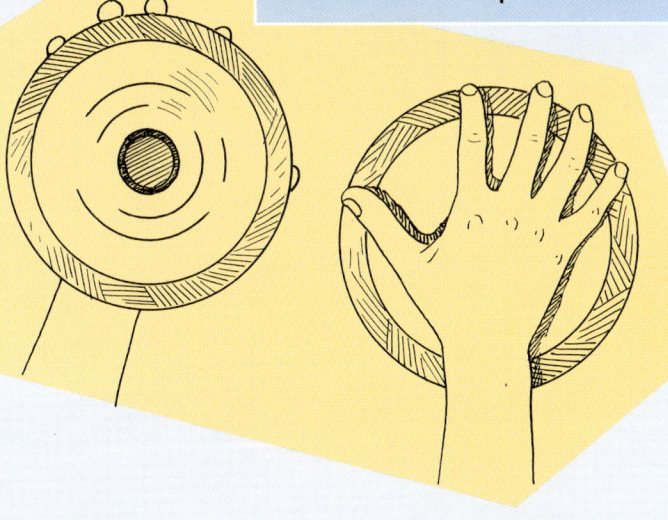

As you prepare to throw, concentrate hard, keeping your eyes on the discus.

Turn your back leg, hips, and then your shoulders as you swing around and up, stretching onto your toes and looking out in the direction you will throw.

At the end of the final swing, release the discus off your index finger so that it spins in a clockwise direction out into the throwing area.

Track and Field

The Field Shot Put

The **shot put** event involves throwing, or "putting," a heavy ball of metal, called a *shot*, from the throwing circle into the throwing area. Putting the shot requires a complete body movement. The power starts in your legs and moves through your body to your arms and fingers, and then finally the shot. Start with the standing throw shown below. Then, once you have mastered it, begin the procedure at the back of the throwing circle. Then side-skip forward to add momentum to your throw.

After throwing, you must leave the throwing circle from the back half.

The standing throw

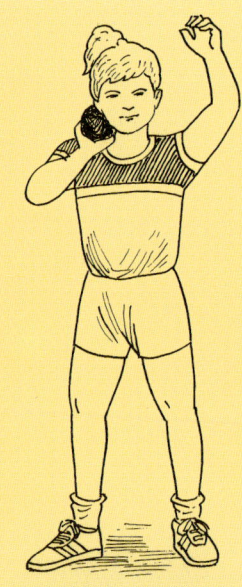

Stand sideways. Place the shot under your chin and close to your neck. Keep your elbow high.

Shift your weight onto your back leg. Bend into it, ready to spring up and around.

Thrust your leading shoulder forward, pushing powerfully off your back leg to turn towards the throwing area.

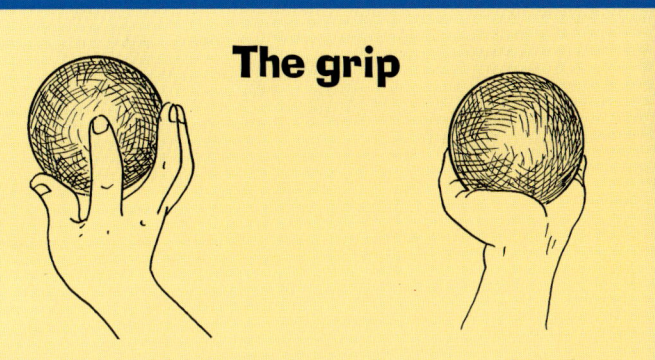

The grip

Hold the shot at the base of your fingers so that three fingers are behind it. Your thumb and little finger hold the shot steady. The shot should not touch your palm.

No part of your body may touch the ground outside the circle during your put. Your toe may touch the inside of the **stop board** but not the top of it. The shot must land in the throwing area.

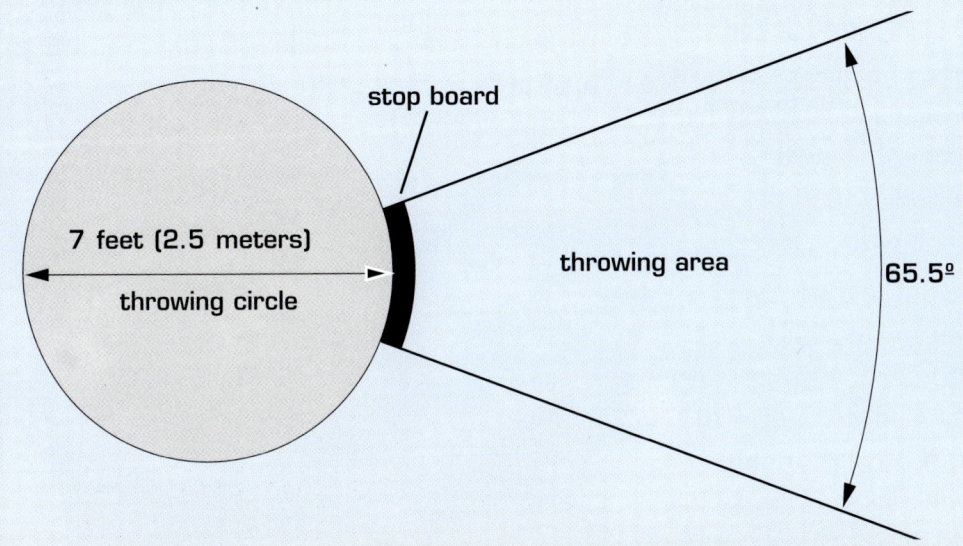

The shot is "put" from a concrete throwing circle which is about 7 feet (2.5 m) in diameter. At the front of this circle is a raised stop board, 4 inches (10 cm) high.

Move your weight onto your front foot as you push the shot upwards and forwards.

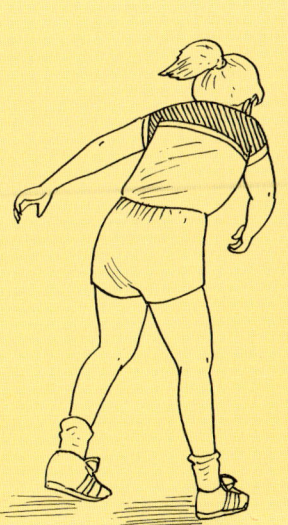

Follow through powerfully – be careful to stay inside the throwing circle!

Track and Field 23

The Field
Long Jump and Triple Jump

Competitors in the **long jump** and **triple jump** try to cover the greatest horizontal distance. The same jumping pit can be used for both jumps, and both have the same take-off rule. You can take off from on or behind the **take-off board**. However, if any part of your foot is over it, a "no jump" results.

The jumps are measured from the part of the mark left in the sand nearest the take-off board. Falling back will result in a shorter jump, so try to bend your knees and push your hips and shoulders forward as you land. Competitors usually make three jumps each—the best one is recorded.

The take off

Your longest jump will come from a fast run-up. When you take off, try to jump upwards as well as forwards with a strong spring from your take-off foot.

long jump

Long jump

The long jump is a single jump from the take-off board into the pit.

Lift your leading knee high as you take off. Stretch your leg forwards and push your arms high into the air.

(24) Top Sport

Triple jump

The triple jump is often called "hop, step, and jump" because that's what it involves.

Practice getting the actions right before you add a fast run-up. Speak through the movement as you practice. Once you have the actions right, concentrate on keeping your hips high, gathering speed and increasing the distance you cover in each phase.

Each phase of the triple jump should be a similar length. Ask a friend to mark your landings and then measure them.

For the hop, land on the same foot you took off from.

Then take a step to land on the other foot.

Spring off to jump, landing in the pit with both feet together.

Push your arms back to help thrust your body forward. As you land, bring your arms forward to help stop you from falling back.

Track and Field 25

The Field High Jump

High jump competitors try to jump the greatest vertical distance. They jump over a bar. The bar is raised a little higher after each round. Competitors who fail to clear a height are out and their best clear jump is recorded. The winner is the one who clears the greatest height.

There are two jumping techniques, The **Fosbury flop** is the most effective style. The **scissor action,** although not used much anymore, is simpler for beginners.

The scissor action

Before moving on to the Fosbury flop, try the scissor action. Set the bar at a height you think you can clear. Stand about 16 feet (5 meters) from the bar, or about nine or ten strides from the bar. Run up to the bar in a curved path so that you approach it sideways. Kick your legs up and over the bar.

the scissor jump

Kick the leg nearest the bar up and over.

Raise your arms for extra lift as your other leg follows.

Land on your bottom on the crash mat.

The Fosbury flop

The Fosbury flop is the most effective method of high jumping. Start with the bar set low and raise it as you improve the technique.

You can try different approach lengths and curves to find the best ones for you. Use your take-off foot, your kicking leg, and your arms to create as much spring as possible for your maximum jump height.

Keep your feet up as your body clears the bar—just a small tap will cause the bar to fall.

the Fosbury flop

Approach the bar in the same way as for the scissor jump. As you take off, start to do a scissor jump, but bend your leading leg.

Turn your shoulders so that your back faces the bar. Arch your back to clear the bar.

Land on the mat on your back.

Track and Field 27

Getting Ready

You should always warm up your muscles and stretch before training or competing. This will prepare your body for activity and help you avoid injury.

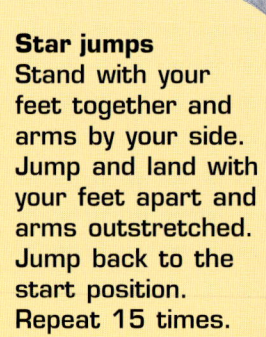

Inner thigh stretch
Stand with your feet wide apart and toes pointing forwards. Rest both hands on one thigh and bend that knee. Keep your back straight. Hold the stretch for a few seconds. Then slowly stand up and stretch to the other side.

Star jumps
Stand with your feet together and arms by your side. Jump and land with your feet apart and arms outstretched. Jump back to the start position. Repeat 15 times.

Arm circles
Stretch your arms up above your head. As you lower them, rotate your arms in small circles.

28 Top Sport

Push-ups
Lie face down on the ground with your hands below your shoulders. Keep your body straight and push up with your arms. Support yourself on the balls of your feet. You can also do push ups with your knees on the ground. Repeat 10 times.

Sit-ups
Lie on your back with your knees bent and hands behind your head. Keep your feet on the ground and sit up using your stomach muscles. Slowly lie down again. Repeat 10 times.

Hurdle stretch
Sit with one leg bent to the side and stretch forward to the other leg. Hold the stretch for a few seconds. Then change position and stretch the other side.

Side bends
Stand with your feet shoulder-width apart and your arms stretched above your head. Keeping yourself centered, bend sideways from the hips. Make sure you don't lean forwards or backwards as you bend. Straighten up and then bend to the other side.

Track and Field 29

Taking It Further

Most cities and towns across the United States sponsor track and field programs. USA Track & Field is the official governing body of the sport. It operates the Junior Olympics. Youngsters from 9–18 are eligible for the program. The program is divided by age: Bantam 9–10, Midget 11–12, Youth 13–14, Intermediate 15–16, and Young Men's and Young Women's 17–18.

USA Track & Field
One Hoosier Dome
Indianapolis, Indiana 46225
☎ (317) 261-0500

Hershey's National Track & Field Youth Program holds meets in all 50 states. The organization is sponsored by the President's Council on Physical Fitness and Sports. Athletes from the ages of 9–14 may participate. Over one million athletes compete each year.

Hershey's National Track & Field Youth Program
P. O. Box 810
Hershey, PA 17033
☎ (800) 468-1714

More Books to Read

Ward, Tony. *Track and Field*. Des Plaines, Ill: Heinemann Library, 1997.

Savage, Jeff. *Running*. Parsippany, NJ: Silver Burdett Press, 1995.

Merrison, Tim. *Field Athletics*. Parsippany, NJ: Silver Burdett Press, 1991.

Wright, Gary. *Track & Field: A Step-By-Step Guide*. Mahwah, NJ: Troll Communications, 1990.

Glossary

acceleration zone area of the track where relay runners may begin running before receiving the **baton**

baton hollow tube that is passed from one runner to the next in **relay** races

changeover zone area of the track where the **baton** must be passed from one **relay** runner to the next

discus metal-weighted disc that is thrown in a field event

Fosbury flop most effective technique for clearing the high jump bar

high jump event in which competitors try to clear a horizontal bar

hurdles race in which runners clear a series of obstacles called hurdles

javelin spearlike object that is thrown in a field event.

long jump horizontal jumping event

race walking event in which competitors walk, keeping at last one foot touching the ground at all times

relay team running event in which a **baton** is passed from runner to runner

scissor action technique for clearing the high jump bar, usually used by beginners

shot put field event in which a metal ball (shot) is thrown (put)

sprint short race in which competitors cover the whole distance at top speed

starting blocks blocks used for **sprint** starts to give sprinters maximum push-off

stop board curved piece of wood at the front edge of the throwing circle for **discus** and **shot put** events, which competitors must not step over

take-off board wooden board at the end of the **long jump** or **triple jump** run up that competitors take off from or behind

throwing area area that the **javelin, discus,** or **shot put** must land in

throwing circle concrete circle from which the **shot put** and **discus** events take place

triple jump jump sequence involving a hop, a step, and a jump

Index

acceleration zone   12
Athens   8

Baron Pierre du Coubertin   9
baton   12, 13

changeover zone   12

dip finish   15
discus   5, 20–21

field events   5, 18–19, 20–21, 22–23, 24–25, 26–27
Fosbury flop   26–27
foul   19

Greece   8
grips   18, 21, 23

high jump   5, 26–27
hop   25
hurdles   5, 14–15

javelin   5, 18–19
jumping events   5, 24–25, 26–27

landing   24–25, 26–27
lanes   5, 10, 12, 16
long distance running   16
long jump   24–25

marathon   5, 6
middle distance running   6, 16

no jump   24

Olympic Games   6–7, 8–9
   Ancient   8, 9
   Modern   6–7, 9
on your marks   10

Pheidippides   8

race walking   17
relays   5, 6, 12–13
running action   11

safety   5, 18
scissor action   26
set   10–11
shoes   11
shot put   5, 9, 22
spikes   11
sprint start   10
sprints   6, 10–11
starting blocks   10
stop board   23

take-off board   24
throwing area   19, 20–21, 23
throwing events   18–19, 20–21, 22–23
track   5
track events   5, 10–17
triple jump   24–25

warm-ups   28–29

JOURNAL

Too Big

DREAM A STORY

Bears Don't Go To School

Senior Author
John J. Pikulski

Senior Coordinating Author
J. David Cooper

Senior Consulting Author
William K. Durr

Coordinating Authors
Kathryn H. Au
M. Jean Greenlaw
Marjorie Y. Lipson
Susan E. Page
Sheila W. Valencia
Karen K. Wixson

Authors
Rosalinda B. Barrera
Edwina Bradley
Ruth P. Bunyan
Jacqueline L. Chaparro
Jacqueline C. Comas
Alan N. Crawford
Robert L. Hillerich
Timothy G. Johnson
Jana M. Mason
Pamela A. Mason
William E. Nagy
Joseph S. Renzulli
Alfredo Schifini

Senior Advisor
Richard C. Anderson

Advisors
Christopher J. Baker
Charles Peters
MaryEllen Vogt

HOUGHTON MIFFLIN COMPANY   BOSTON

Atlanta   Dallas   Geneva, Illinois   Palo Alto   Princeton   Toronto

1995 Impression
Copyright © 1993 by Houghton Mifflin Company. All rights reserved.

Permission is hereby granted to teachers to reprint or photocopy in classroom quantities the pages or sheets in this work that carry a Houghton Mifflin Company copyright notice. These pages are designed to be reproduced by teachers for use in their classes with accompanying Houghton Mifflin material, provided each copy made shows the copyright notice. Such copies may not be sold and further distribution is expressly prohibited. Except as authorized above, prior written permission must be obtained from Houghton Mifflin Company to reproduce or transmit this work or portions thereof in any other form or by any other electronic or mechanical means, including any information storage or retrieval system, unless expressly permitted by federal copyright law. Address inquiries to School Permissions, Houghton Mifflin Company, 222 Berkeley Street, Boston, MA 02116.

Printed in the U.S.A.   ISBN: 0-395-61964-5   89-WC-96

CONTENTS

Too Big

THEME 1: Animal Friends

- Introducing the Theme — 1
- The Writing Center — 2
  - *Skip to My Lou* — 3
  - *Who Is Tapping At My Window?* — 9
  - *Dear Zoo* — 13
  - *My Friends* — 17

THEME 2: I Can Do It!

- Introducing the Theme — 19
- The Writing Center — 20
  - *I Can't Get My Turtle to Move* — 21
  - *I Wish I Could Fly* — 26
  - *Monster and the Baby* — 31
  - *Bet You Can't* — 33

Dream a Story

THEME 1: Wild Animals, Come Out!

- Introducing the Theme — 35
- The Writing Center — 36
  - *Monkeys in the Jungle* — 37
  - *Listen to the Desert* — 41
  - *Sophie and Jack* — 45
  - *Have You Seen the Crocodile?* — 50

THEME 2: Friends Near and Far

- Introducing the Theme — 53
- The Writing Center — 54
  - *I Need a Friend* — 55
  - *A Playhouse for Monster* — 60
  - *School Days* — 67
  - *Toby in the Country, Toby in the City* — 71

CONTENTS

Bears Don't Go to School

THEME 1: Working Together

❏ Introducing the Theme	73
❏ The Writing Center	74
Potluck	78
Raking Leaves	85
Sophie and Jack Help Out	88
Bones, Bones, Dinosaur Bones	93

THEME 2: Something Special

❏ Introducing the Theme	95
❏ The Writing Center	96
My Brown Bear Barney	100
If I Had a Pig	104
I Need a Lunch Box	108
Daniel Goes Fishing	113

Reading on My Own — 115

Spelling Guide — 119

Animal Friends
_____
_____
by _____

Introducing the Theme
Responding
Children draw the animal friends they are most looking forward to reading about. They should write their names in the space provided.

The Writing Center

The Writing Center: Telling About an Animal Friend

Children draw a picture of an animal friend. Then they write a label or caption for the picture.

Skip, skip, skip to my Lou!

Skip, skip, skip to my Lou!

ANIMAL FRIENDS

Skip to My Lou
Responding

Children draw a picture of their favorite animal friend or event from *Skip to My Lou*. They may caption their pictures.

Skip to My Lou
Responding
Using part of the selection verse, children think of words to add in the blank spaces. Then they complete the first lines and read the completed verse.

_____

_____

in the
_____

_____

What'll I do?

Skip to my Lou, my darling!

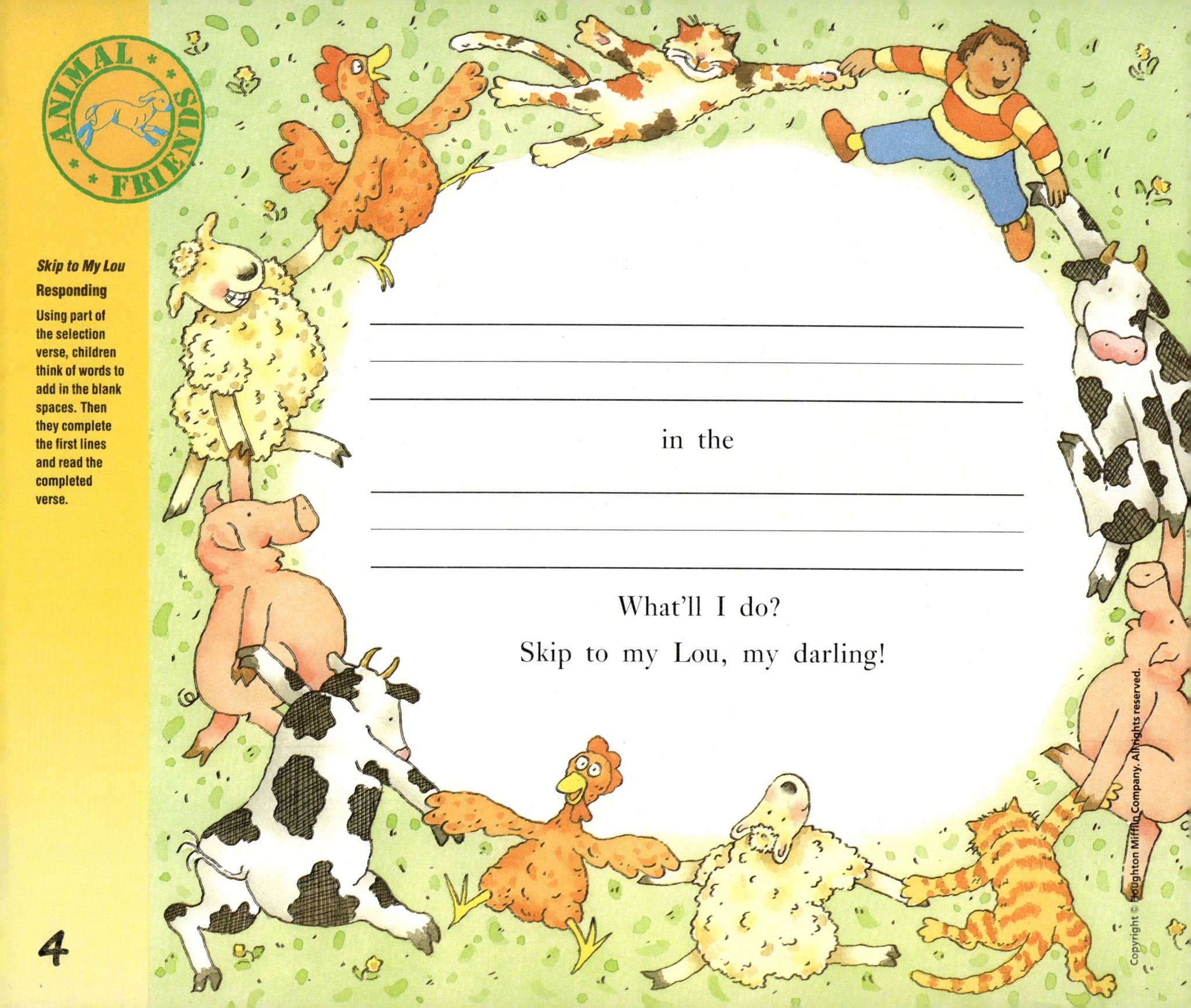

p   r   l

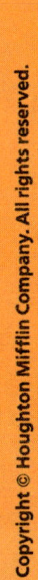

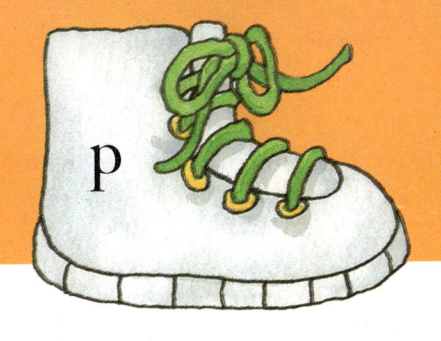

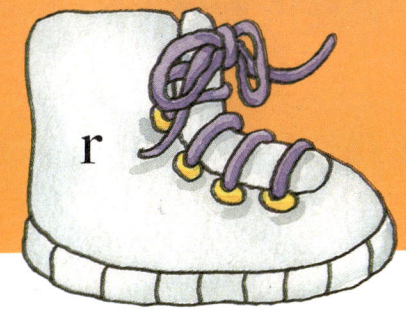

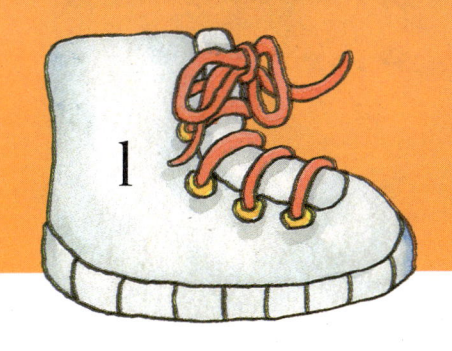

Can You Run, Baby Bear?

____
____
Mother ____et Baby Bear run.

____
____
Baby Bear ____an to the can.

____   ____
____   ____
Baby Bear ____an to the ____ot.

____   ____
____   ____
Baby Bear ____an and ____an.

____   ____
____   ____
Baby Bear ____an a ____ot!

***Skip to My Lou*
Phonics**

Children complete the sentences in the story by adding the initial consonant in each blank space, choosing from the listed letters. Then children may read the story aloud.

5

Skip to My Lou
Responding
Children list words from *Skip to My Lou* that they especially want to remember. These could be words that interest them or words they found difficult.

My Words

	bear	
cat		pig
	dog	

Skip to My Lou
Vocabulary
Children cut out the cards and match the name of each "animal friend" with its picture by pasting the two cards together back-to-back. With their new cards, children may play games such as Spell-a-Friend: One child shows the picture side to a partner, who then spells the word.

8

m g d
   c
p h
r

____ooster

"Good ____orning!"

____oat

____ig

____orse

____onkey

____ow

Who Is Tapping at My Window?
Phonics
Children say the name of each animal and then add the first letter of that animal name, choosing from the letters listed above. Then children may finish the sentence.

ANIMAL FRIENDS

Who Is Tapping At My Window?

Responding

Children think of animals other than those named in the story to complete the responses to the question. Then they can, if they wish, draw the new animals.

Who is tapping at my window?

_____

_____

"It's not I," said the _____ .

_____

_____

"It's not I," said the _____ .

_____

_____

"It's not I," said the _____ .

Who Is Tapping at My Window?
Writing

Children may choose a favorite farm animal, draw a picture of it, and write a label or a sentence to go with the picture. Then they cut out the page and write their names on the back. The pages can be bound together in a class book.

11

by

From all your friends at the zoo.

Dear Zoo
Responding
Children recall which pets were sent back to the zoo and choose one animal they would have kept. Children draw a picture of that animal and tell why they would have kept it.

s y f t z k

____angaroo

____iger

____ebra

____ak

____ox

____eal

More pets from the ____oo!

Dear Zoo
Phonics
Tell children that here are some more "zoo pets" that could have been sent to the child in the story. Children say the name of each animal and then add the first letter of that animal name, choosing from the letters listed above. Then they may finish the word in the caption below.

14

I wrote to the _____ to send me a pet.
They sent me a _____.
It was _____.
So I _____.

Dear Zoo
Responding
Using sentence patterns from the selection, children think of other words to add in the blank spaces to create new stories. Then they share their stories with others.

15

Dear Zoo
Phonics
Children choose and write the word that completes each rhyme and goes with the picture. (Not all words will be used.) Children may then read the verses aloud.

pet   bit   quit   sun   pot   fan

I wrote to **Nan** _____
To send me a _____.

I wrote to **Dot** _____
To send me a _____.

I wrote to the **vet** _____
To send me a _____.

I wrote to **Kit**. _____
Now it's time to _____!

16

| hurry up in the morning | be good to my pets |
| know what time it is | have fun |

I learned to _____

from _____.

| my mother | my father | my pet | my friend |

My Friends

Vocabulary/ Language Patterns

Children create stories about what they have learned from friends and family. They may choose from the suggested phrases or use their own. Then they may illustrate their stories.

1. Go to my friend the **zebra**.
2. Now go to my friend the **hippo**.
3. Now go to my friend the **mouse**.

Did you get a star?

My Friends

Reading New Words

Children read the directions on this page, using the initial consonant sound, the meaning of the sentence, and the pictures to help them figure out each word in heavy, dark type. Then, with the teacher's help, they begin at the picture of the pencil and draw lines according to the directions.

I can do it!

I can ride!

I can write!

I Can Do It!

by _____

Introducing the Theme
Responding

Children decide which story they most want to read, and draw a picture of themselves doing something that a character in that story is doing. Then children write their names in the space provided.

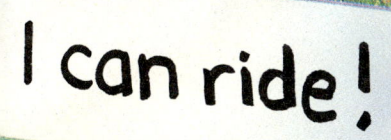

The Writing Center

The Writing Center: Something You Would Like to Do

Children think of something they want to learn to do. Then they draw a picture and dictate or write a sentence about that activity.

I Can't Get My Turtle to Move

Responding

Children respond by drawing or writing an answer to one or both of these questions: How did the girl get her turtle to move? What would *you* have done?

I CAN DO IT!

I Can't Get My Turtle to Move
Responding

Children draw the animal they liked most in the story. Then they complete the sentence with a command they might give such an animal. They may use words from the story or other words if they wish.

"_____," I say, and they do.

22

m n p t

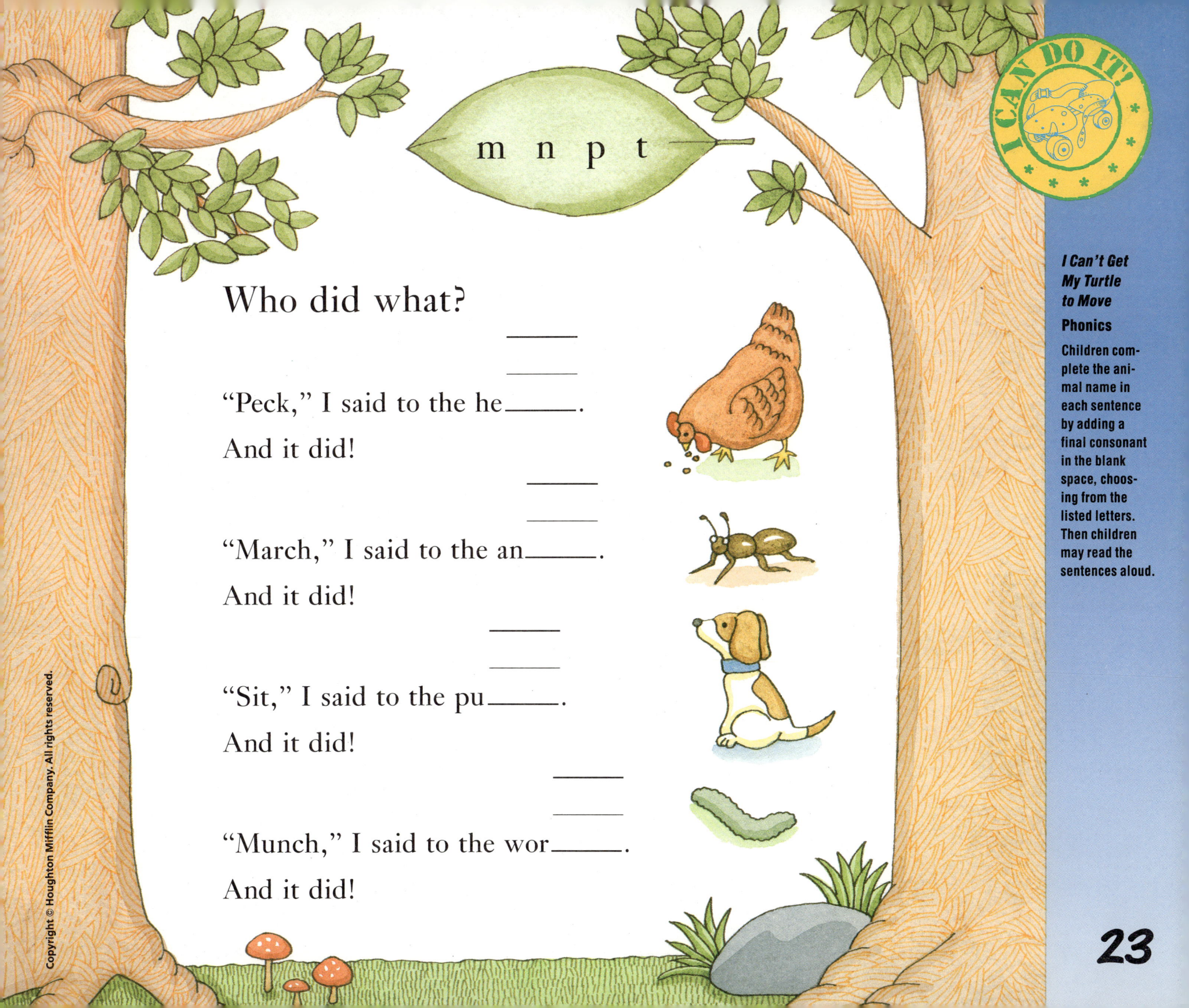

Who did what?

"Peck," I said to the he_____.
And it did!

"March," I said to the an_____.
And it did!

"Sit," I said to the pu_____.
And it did!

"Munch," I said to the wor_____.
And it did!

I Can't Get My Turtle to Move
Phonics
Children complete the animal name in each sentence by adding a final consonant in the blank space, choosing from the listed letters. Then children may read the sentences aloud.

My Words

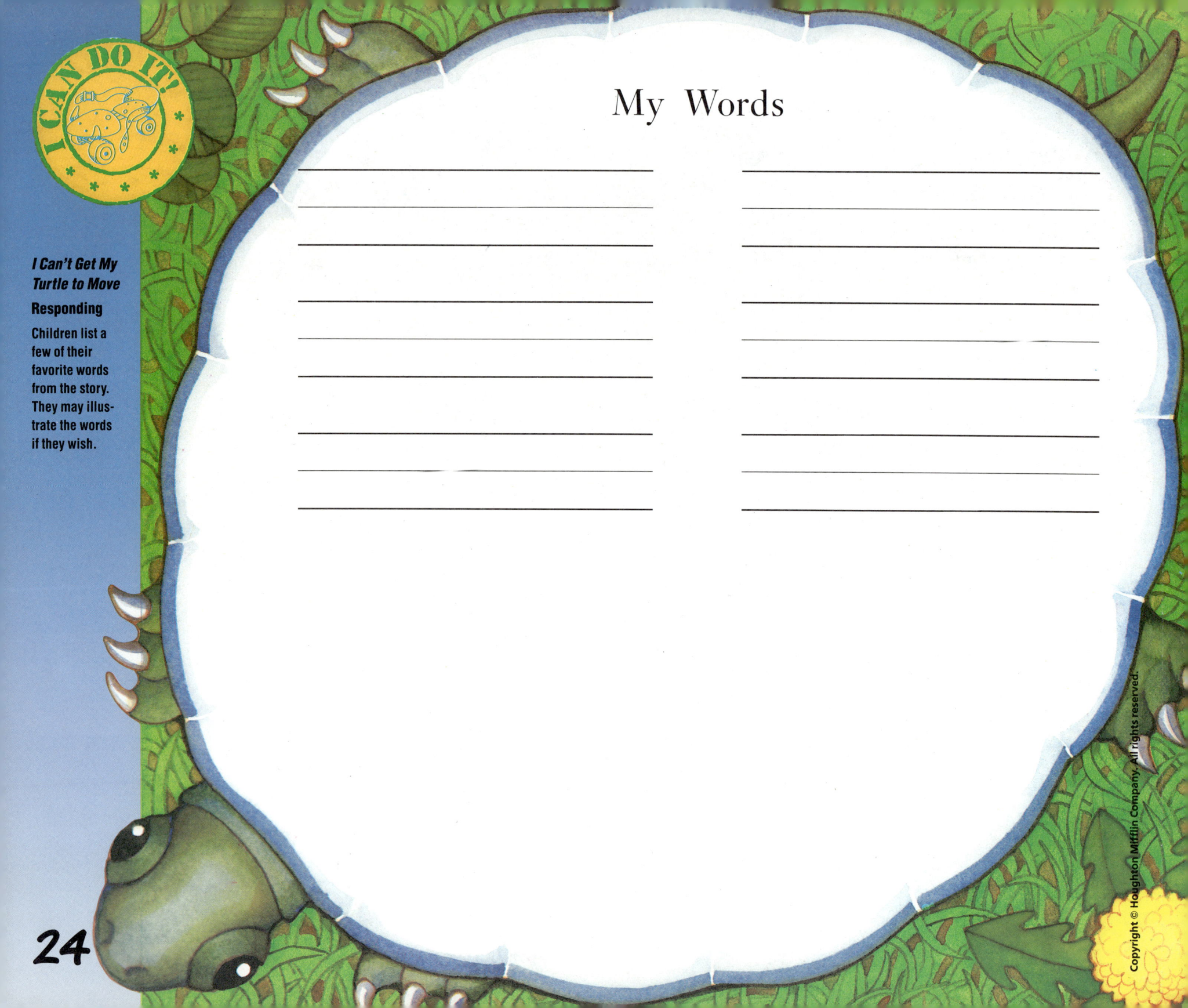

I Can't Get My Turtle to Move

Responding

Children list a few of their favorite words from the story. They may illustrate the words if they wish.

STORY STARTER

One day, Rabbit was talking to Turtle.

"I have to run now," said Rabbit.

"What is your hurry, Rabbit?" said Turtle.

I Can Do It!

I Can't Get My Turtle to Move
Vocabulary

Children read the story starter, reviewing some of the high-frequency words they have learned in this theme. Then they illustrate the scene in the space above it. Children may want to continue the story on other paper.

I CAN DO IT!

n t g l

Turtle said, "I can't fly like a bird,

dive like a fro___,

climb like a squirre___,

or ru___ like a rabbi___.
But...

I don't get we___ in the rai___!"

I Wish I Could Fly

Phonics

Children complete the sentences about the story by adding a final consonant in each blank space, choosing from the listed letters. Then children may read the sentences aloud.

26

"Good morning, _____.
I wish I could fly like you."

"Hello, _____.
I wish I could dive like you."

"Good day, _____.
I wish I could run like you."

I Wish I Could Fly
Responding
Children choose animal names other than those in the story to complete the sentences. Then they may draw the new animals.

**I Wish
I Could Fly
Phonics**

Children complete the sentences by adding the final consonant or consonants in each blank space, choosing from the listed letters. Then children read the sentences aloud.

28

x   rr   zz   ss

You Can!

You can bu_____ like a bee.

You can pu_____ like a cat.

You can ki_____ like a dog.

You can run like a fo_____.

Three cats climb.
Cats like to climb.

Two cats jump.
Cats like to jump.

This bird can fly now.
Do you wish you could?

This bird can't fly now.
But it will!

I Wish I Could Fly
Vocabulary
Children read each sentence pair and decide which picture goes with it. They cut out the pictures and, after rereading each sentence pair to be sure, they paste the pictures next to the matching text.

I CAN DO IT!

Monster and the Baby

Responding

Children respond by drawing and/or writing an answer to this question: What makes *you* laugh?

31

Monster and the Baby

Responding

Using sentence patterns from the selection, children think of other toys that Monster could have used. Children complete the sentences and share them with others. They may also draw the toys.

Monster gave Baby a _____.
Baby cried.

Monster gave Baby a _____.
Baby cried.

Monster gave Baby a _____.
Baby laughed and laughed.

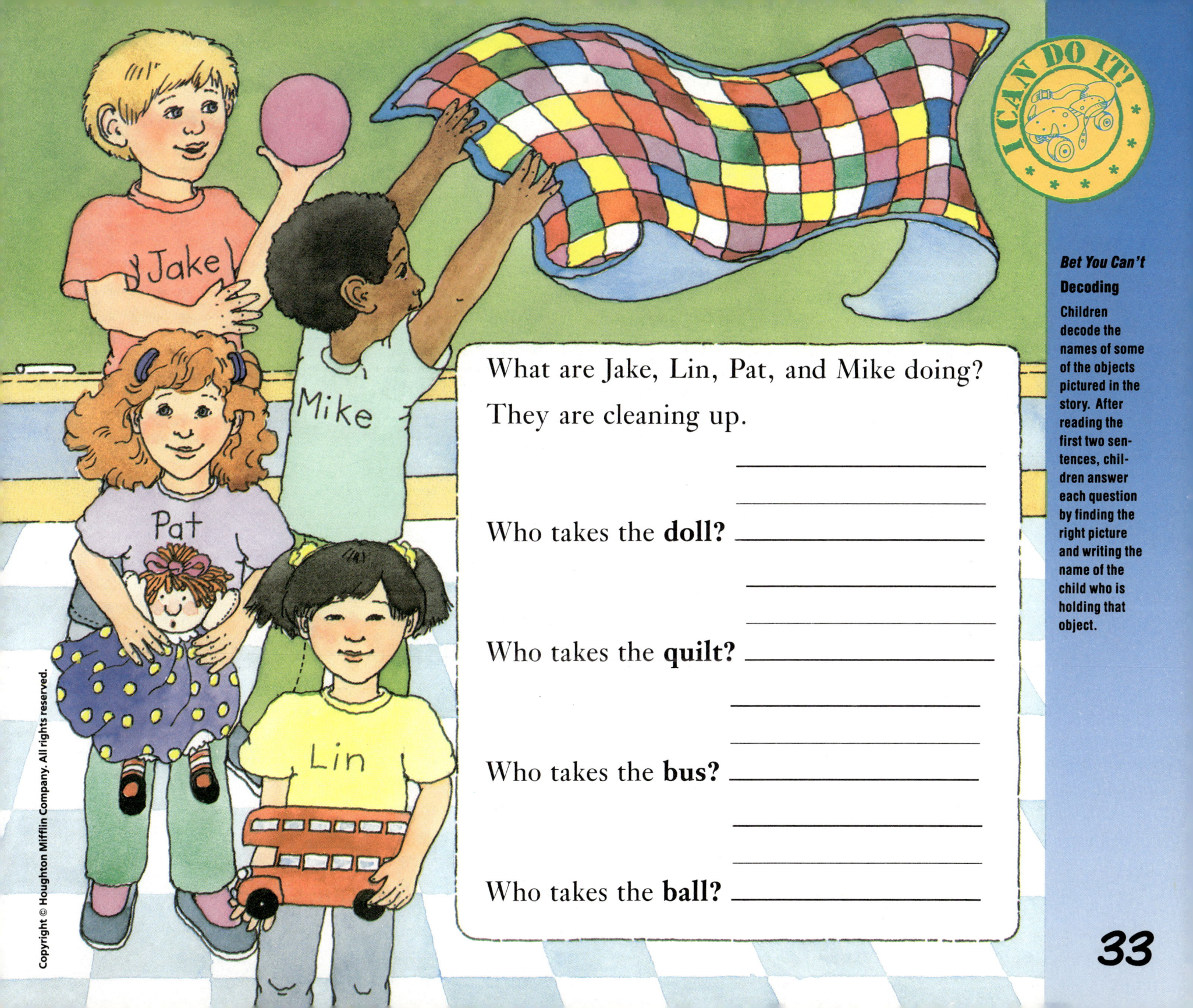

What are Jake, Lin, Pat, and Mike doing?
They are cleaning up.

Who takes the **doll?** _____

Who takes the **quilt?** _____

Who takes the **bus?** _____

Who takes the **ball?** _____

Bet You Can't Decoding
Children decode the names of some of the objects pictured in the story. After reading the first two sentences, children answer each question by finding the right picture and writing the name of the child who is holding that object.

33

I CAN DO IT!

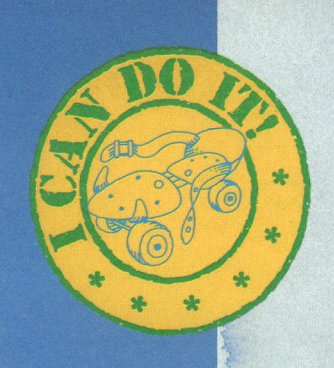

Bet You Can't Vocabulary

Children choose and write a word from the list to complete each sentence. (Accept any response that makes sense.) Children may illustrate one or more of their sentences.

Can you do it?
Bet you can!

guess   book   laugh   walk

You can read a _____.

You can _____ what time it is.

You can _____ like a duck.

You can _____ and have fun.

34

Wild Animals, Come Out!

by _____

Introducing the Theme

Responding

Children decide which wild animal or animals they most want to read about. Have children pretend they are taking a picture of that wild animal, and have them draw the photo they would take. Children may also write their names in the space provided.

The Writing Center

The Writing Center: Your Wild Animal Story

Children create a fantasy animal — a storybook or cartoon character, or an animal with parts from different animals they have read about. Children then dictate or write about that animal.

Monkeys in the Jungle

Responding

Have children respond to this question: If you could be one of the animals in this story, which one would you be? Have children draw and label it and tell why they would like to be that animal.

Monkeys in the Jungle
Responding
Children read and then correct the "silly sentences" by writing the correct animal name in each blank.

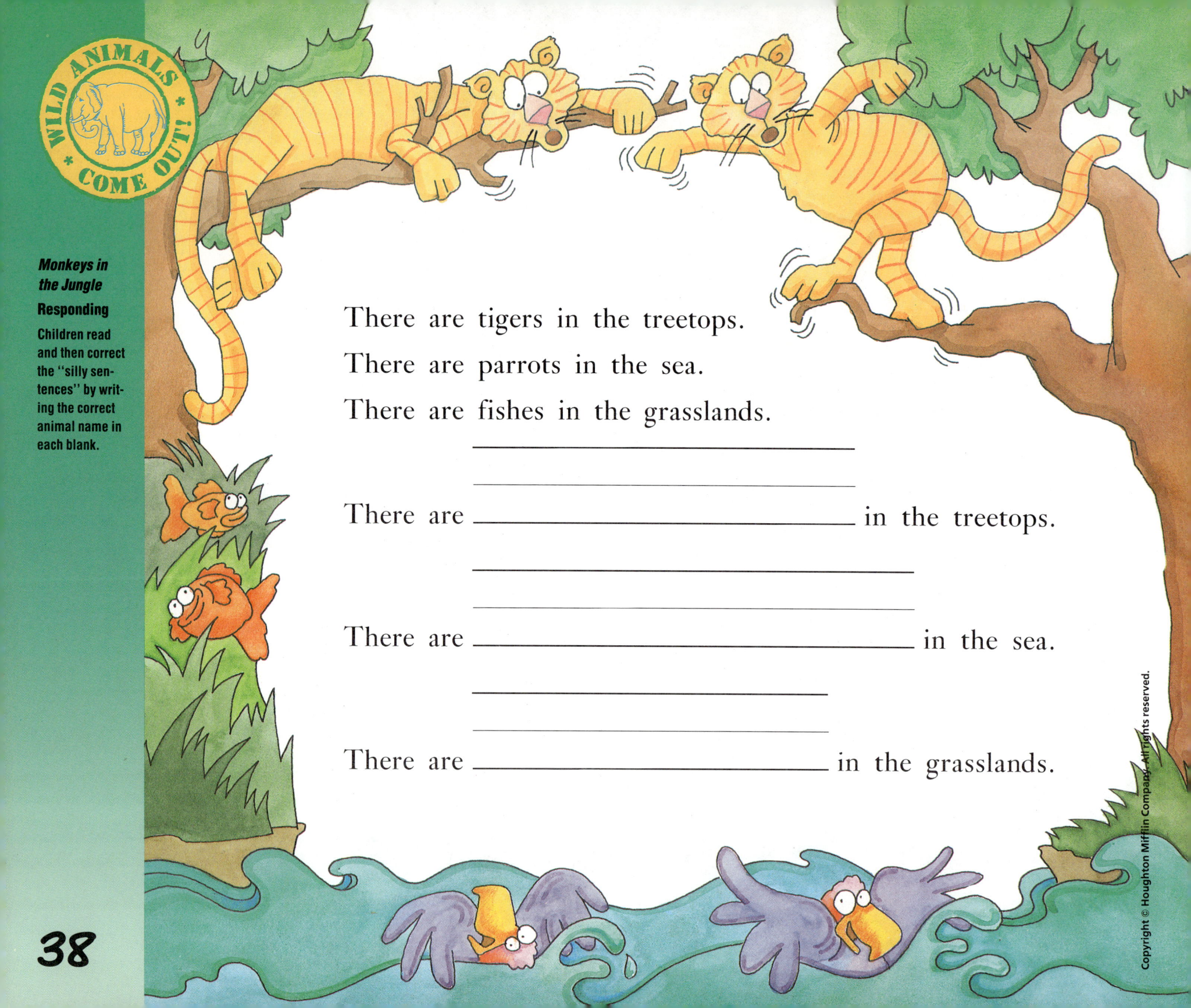

There are tigers in the treetops.
There are parrots in the sea.
There are fishes in the grasslands.

There are _____ in the treetops.

There are _____ in the sea.

There are _____ in the grasslands.

38

Here are all the animals walking in a row.

Here come the ducks.
They are talking.
There is the elephant.
Where is the bird?
It's up there on the elephant!

_____
_____

The ducks are walking and _____.

_____
_____

The bird is on the _____.

Monkeys in the Jungle Vocabulary

Children read the story, which contains many of the new high-frequency words practiced in this theme. Then they complete the sentences about the story.

WILD ANIMALS COME OUT!

39

Some Words I Like

Monkeys in the Jungle
Responding
Children list some words from the story that they would like to save for their own writing.

40

On the ground | In the air | In the water

Listen to the Desert Responding

Point out that the animals in *Listen to the Desert* can be found in different parts of the desert. Read the captions on this page. Then children choose one animal from *Listen to the Desert* that belongs in each category and draw the animal in that space.

41

ch   th

One, two, three, four, five,
_____
_____
Once I caught a _____imp alive.

Six, seven, eight, nine, ten,
_____
_____
_____en I let it go again!

_____
_____
See it mar_____
_____
_____
on the pa_____,

_____
_____
Then that _____imp
_____
_____
will take a ba_____!

I Caught a Fish

Phonics

Using the pictures as clues, children add *ch* or *th* to complete the words in the verse. Then children read the verse aloud together.

42

Listen to the _____ say,

_____ , _____ , _____ !

Listen to the _____ say,

_____ , _____ , _____ !

Listen to the Desert Responding

Using sentence patterns from the selection, children fill in the blanks with names of things that make noise and then make up words to represent the sounds the things make. Encourage imaginative responses.

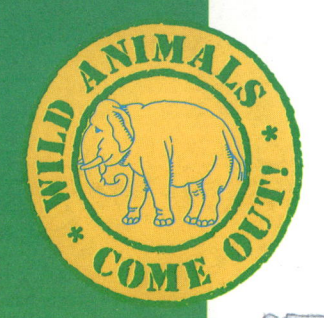

Name the Book

-ish   -ut   -en

WILD ANIMALS COME OUT!

Listen to the Desert
Phonics
Children choose and write the phonogram to complete one word in each book title. Children may then write a story based on one of the titles.

Three M_____ on the Elephant

Monkeys in a H_____

Cat Gets a F_____

H_____ Is the Best!

44

Sophie and Jack
Responding

Ask children what kind of animals Sophie and Jack were. Then have them draw and/or write an answer to this question: What would have been some good hiding places for Sophie and Jack if they had been frogs instead of hippos?

Sophie and Jack
Phonics

After using what they have learned about phonograms to read the words in the box, children read each sentence and write the word that belongs in the blank. Children may then read the story aloud.

ride   hid   did   lid

"Here comes Lion," said Monkey. "Let's hide."

Monkey _____ in the can.

Frog hid in the _____.

Elephant _____ not hide.

Elephant said to Lion, "Would you

like a _____?"

46

WILD ANIMALS COME OUT!

Sophie and Jack

Writing

Children may contribute pages to a class Hippo Shape Book. They cut out the page and then write descriptive words or a sentence telling something they like about hippos. Children then write their names on the back.

by
_____
_____
_____

ch sh th

____ump! ____ump!

spla____! spla____!

ou____! ou____!

cra____! cra____!

Sophie and Jack
Phonics
Tell children that here are some other animals that are trying to hide like Sophie and Jack, but that they make noises that give them away. Children add *ch, sh,* or *th* to complete each "sound word."

Have You Seen the Crocodile?

Decoding

Using the list below the sentences, children decode each new animal name and write that word in the space beside its picture. Then children read the completed sentence aloud.

Have you seen the crocodile?

No,

_____
said the _____

and the _____

and the _____

and the _____.

| bat | chicken | fish | sheep |

50

Who Are We?

We are in a play.

We are taking a walk.

We are going to teach.

We get up in the spring.

Have You Seen the Crocodile?
Vocabulary

Children read each sentence and decide which picture goes with it. They cut out the pictures and, after rereading each sentence to be sure, they paste the pictures below the matching text.

FRIENDS NEAR AND FAR

Friends Near and Far

by _____

Introducing the Theme

Responding

Children choose an activity they most want to read about and perhaps do with their own friends. Children then draw "snapshots" and write their names in the space provided.

The Writing Center

The Writing Center: Tell About a Friend

Children draw a picture of a good friend. Then they dictate or write something about that friend.

I Need a Friend

Responding

Ask children how they think the girl felt at the end of the story. Children then draw a picture of the girl and dictate or write a sentence about what made her happy.

FRIENDS NEAR AND FAIR

I Need a Friend
Responding

Using the sentence patterns from the selection, children think of other words to add in the blank spaces to create new stories. (The pictures may help give them ideas.) Then children share their stories with others.

All by myself _____
_____

I can _____ .

But I need a friend _____
_____

to _____ .

56

We are friends who like to draw.

Trish draws a **truck**.

Bruce draws a **bridge**.

Craig draws a **crocodile**.

Fred draws a **frog**.

I Need a Friend
Phonics

With the teacher's help, children read the character names and other words in heavy, dark type. They cut out the pictures and paste each one beside the sentence that describes it. Children may use the back of the sheet to draw other pictures whose names begin with a cluster with *r* and label them.

58

My Words to Keep

**I Need a Friend
Responding**

Children make a list of words from the story that they want to "keep" for their own writing.

FRIENDS NEAR AND FAR

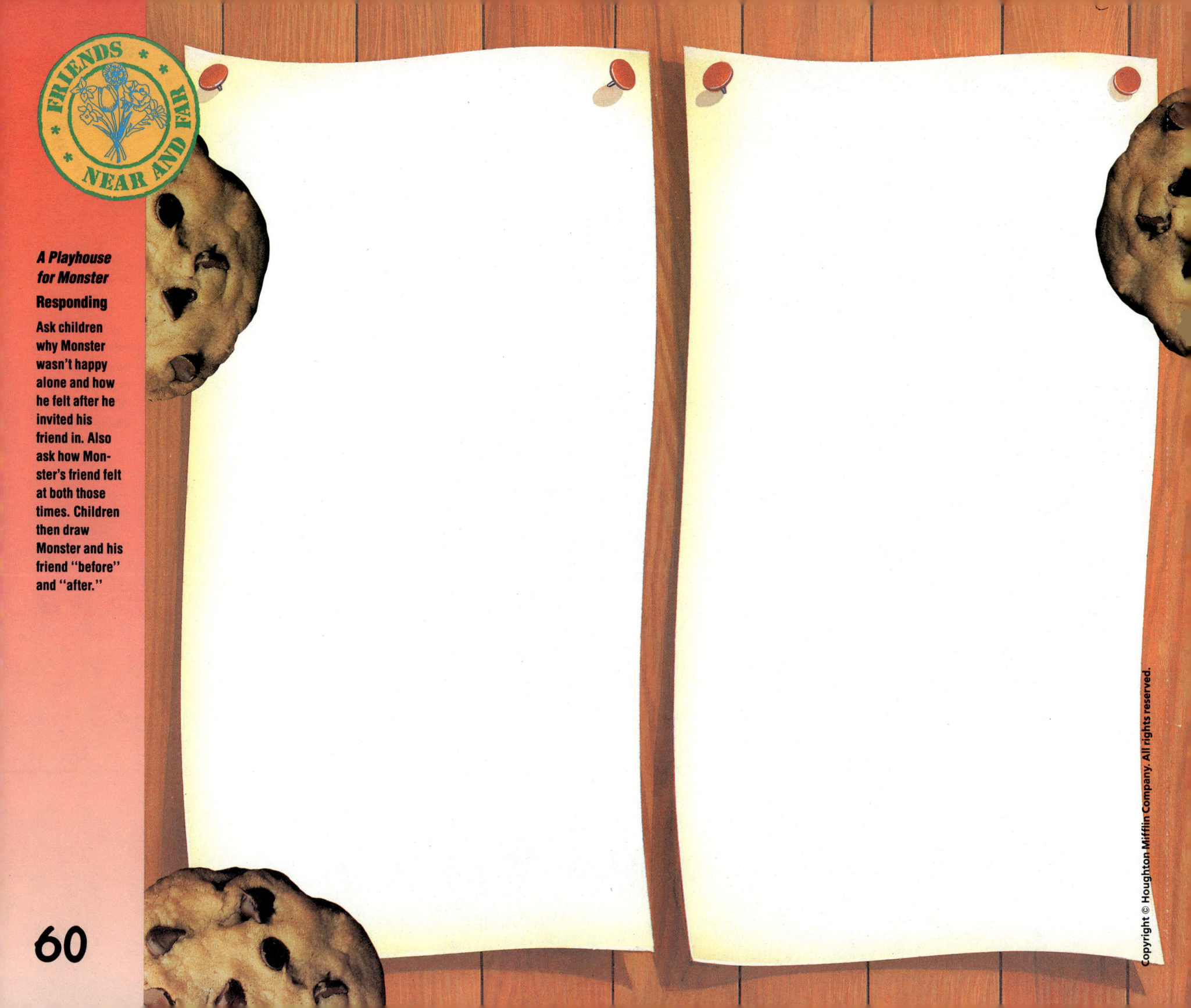

A Playhouse for Monster

Responding

Ask children why Monster wasn't happy alone and how he felt after he invited his friend in. Also ask how Monster's friend felt at both those times. Children then draw Monster and his friend "before" and "after."

60

Copyright © Houghton Mifflin Company. All rights reserved.

Monster and his friend could play with...

sled	flute	blanket
plane	blocks	glue

A Playhouse for Monster

Phonics

Children look at the pictures and use what they know about consonant clusters to help them read the labels. They choose a label to go with each picture and print it in the lines.

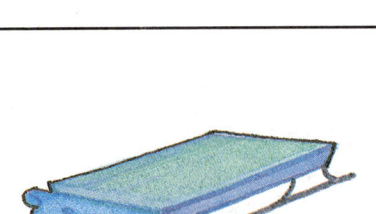

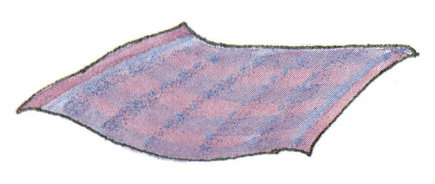

of friend for give

A Playhouse for Monster
Vocabulary
Children read each sentence, then choose a word from the box to complete it so that it tells about the picture. They may want to tell how the sentences are alike and different.

Here's a picture _____ a friend.

Here's a picture _____ a friend.

I'll _____ this to the cat.

I'll give a cat _____ to my _____.

62

"This is my room," Monster said.

"These are my _____."

"This is my _____."

"These are my _____."

"Welcome!"

A Playhouse for Monster
Responding

Children fill in the pattern with the names of things Monster might have in his bedroom. Then they draw a picture to show Monster sharing one of these things with a friend. Children may also read their completed sentences aloud.

63

FRIENDS NEAR AND FAR

A Playhouse for Monster
Phonics

On this page, children make block puzzles—something that Monster and his friend might do in the playhouse. Children use the clues to fill in the puzzles, choosing from the words above the clues. Children may then want to make similar puzzles on other paper, using words that end with *-eed*, *-ell*, and *-est*.

feed   tell

1. To talk: _____
2. One thing you do for a pet: _____ it

yell   rest

3. What you do when you shout: _____
4. What you do when you are sleeping: _____

nest   seed

5. What you need for this 🌸 _____
6. The best birdhouse of all: _____

64

My friend Ed and I like elephants.

1. Ed and I have races.
   We run like elephants.

2. We like to laugh.
   We tell elephant jokes.

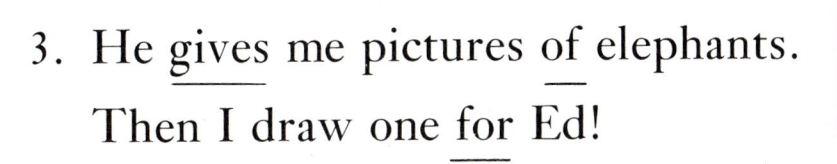

3. He gives me pictures of elephants.
   Then I draw one for Ed!

A Playhouse for Monster
Vocabulary
Children read each sentence pair and decide which picture goes with it. They cut out the pictures and paste each one next to its matching text.

65

FRIENDS NEAR AND FAR

School Days
Responding

Children recall some of the special school experiences shown in the story, such as whole-class art projects, a fire drill, and someone losing a front tooth. Children then draw a picture of something they and their friends have enjoyed and add a caption.

_____

_____

_____

School Days
Phonics
After reading the rhyme at the top, children choose and add the correct cluster in each blank space. Children may then read all the sentences aloud.

When school is out, we play and shout!

sk   sl   sm   sn   st   sw

We go on the ____ings.

We ____ate on the walk.

At times, we play in the ____ow.

We all ____ile and laugh.

Come on in and take a look,
_____
_____

We will _____ .

We can dance, we can sing,
_____
_____

We can _____ .

Now it's time to go and play.
_____
_____

We will _____ .

School Days
Responding

Using patterns similar to those in the story, children complete sentences to tell their own school stories. Though children may finish the sentences as they wish, encourage them to try to make the second line rhyme with the first.

School Days
Phonics

With the teacher's help, children read the sentences in the speech balloon. Then they choose and write the phonogram that completes the words in each rhyme, using the picture to help them. Children may then think of other rhymes the two friends might make up.

70

We like to rhyme.
We have a good time!

-am   -ame   -oke

Ann is my n_____.

My name is the s_____.

It was no j_____.

The day that this br_____.

Here I _____,

Taking the j_____.

Toby in the City · Toby in the Country

flowers   both   beach   leaves

The two Tobys go to the _____ .

They play in the _____ .

They see _____ in the spring.

The two friends _____ have the name Toby.

FRIENDS NEAR AND FAIR

Toby in the Country, Toby in the City
Decoding
Children read each sentence and look at the accompanying picture. They choose a word to complete the sentence and write it in the lines. Children may want to write other sentences about the two Tobys on a sheet of paper and ask classmates to read them.

Dancing · Laughing · Singing

Telling Jokes · Drawing

FRIENDS NEAR AND FAIR

Toby in the Country, Toby in the City

Vocabulary

Children create and illustrate their own stories about things they like to do with friends. They may use the words on the page for ideas.

Sometimes I feel like
___
___
___
___
___
___

72

Helping Out

Working Together

by _____

Introducing the Theme
Responding
Children decide which story they most want to read and draw a picture of themselves working together with the characters. Then they write their names on the lines.

73

The Writing Center

My Helping Surprise

The Writing Center

After talking about their own experiences, children draw the beginning of a story about how they surprised someone by helping them. Then they write or tell about the pictures they drew.

Beginning

Middle

My Helping Surprise

The Writing Center

Children draw their ideas for the middle of their story about helping someone. Then they write or tell about the pictures.

75

My Helping Surprise

The Writing Center

Children draw a picture of the end of their story. Then they write or tell about their pictures.

End

76

My Helping Surprise

My Helping Surprise

The Writing Center

Children review the beginning, the middle, and the end of their story. Then they draw and tell or write about their helping surprises. They share the completed story with friends or family.

Potluck
Responding
Children think about all the foods mentioned in the story. They choose their favorite dishes or the new ones that they look forward to trying, draw pictures of them on the table, and add appropriate labels on the lines (e.g., *Don's dumplings* and *the triplets' tacos*).

My name is _____,

and I'll take _____.

Potluck
Responding
Children pretend that they are invited to the potluck. They write their name on the first line and then complete the sentence with the name of a food that has the same beginning letter. (Example: My name is *Jo,* and I'll take *juice.*) Invite children to illustrate their responses and share them with the class.

van   cab   path   crab

The black dog runs up the _____.

The rabbit comes in a _____.

The fat cats come in a _____.

The turtle walks with the _____.

Potluck
Phonics
Children read the sentences about some animal characters who are going to a potluck supper. Using the picture clues, children decode the short *a* words at the top and write one to complete each sentence. Children then read the sentences aloud.

80

Food I Like Best

Working Together

Potluck
Writing
Children may contribute pages to a class Potluck Shape Book. They cut out the page and then write the names of favorite foods and illustrate them. Children then write their names on the back.

by
_____
_____
_____

Working Words

Potluck
Responding
Children list words from *Potluck* that they would like to remember for reading and writing. (Suggest that they choose words they especially liked, even if they found them difficult at first.)

Potluck

Vocabulary

Children read the story, which contains many of the high-frequency words from this theme. Then they complete the sentences about the story.

Mmmmmm! What could that be?

It was wonderful bread!
Little Bear zoomed in to get some.

Mother Bear laughed and said,
"I finally know how to get you up
in the morning, Little Bear!"

Mother Bear made wonderful _____.

She _____ knows how to get
Little Bear up in the morning.

84

Raking Leaves
Responding
Ask: What happened after Punky jumped into the big pile of leaves on the tarp? Children draw pictures to show what happened after that.

85

tape   rake   game   cake

Raking Leaves
Phonics
Children write the correct word in each sentence, using the words listed. Then children may read the sentences aloud.

Punky and Grampy have fun.
_____

They _____ the leaves.

They put _____ in a book.

They bake a _____ .

Then they play a _____ .

86

I worked hard at being helpful.
_____
_____

I helped to _____ .

Sometimes the _____
_____
_____
went onto the _____ ,
and sometimes it didn't.

Raking Leaves
Responding
Children fill in the blanks to write "helping-out" stories about themselves. Children may then illustrate their stories.

WORKING TOGETHER

Sophie and Jack Help Out

Responding

Ask: What happened after Sophie and Jack planted the seeds? Then what happened after the big rainstorm? Children draw a favorite part of the story and write or tell whether it happened at the beginning, the middle, or the end.

88

Dad and I made
a doghouse.

Dad and I did
housework.

Dad and I made
a birdhouse.

Dad made a plaything
just for me.

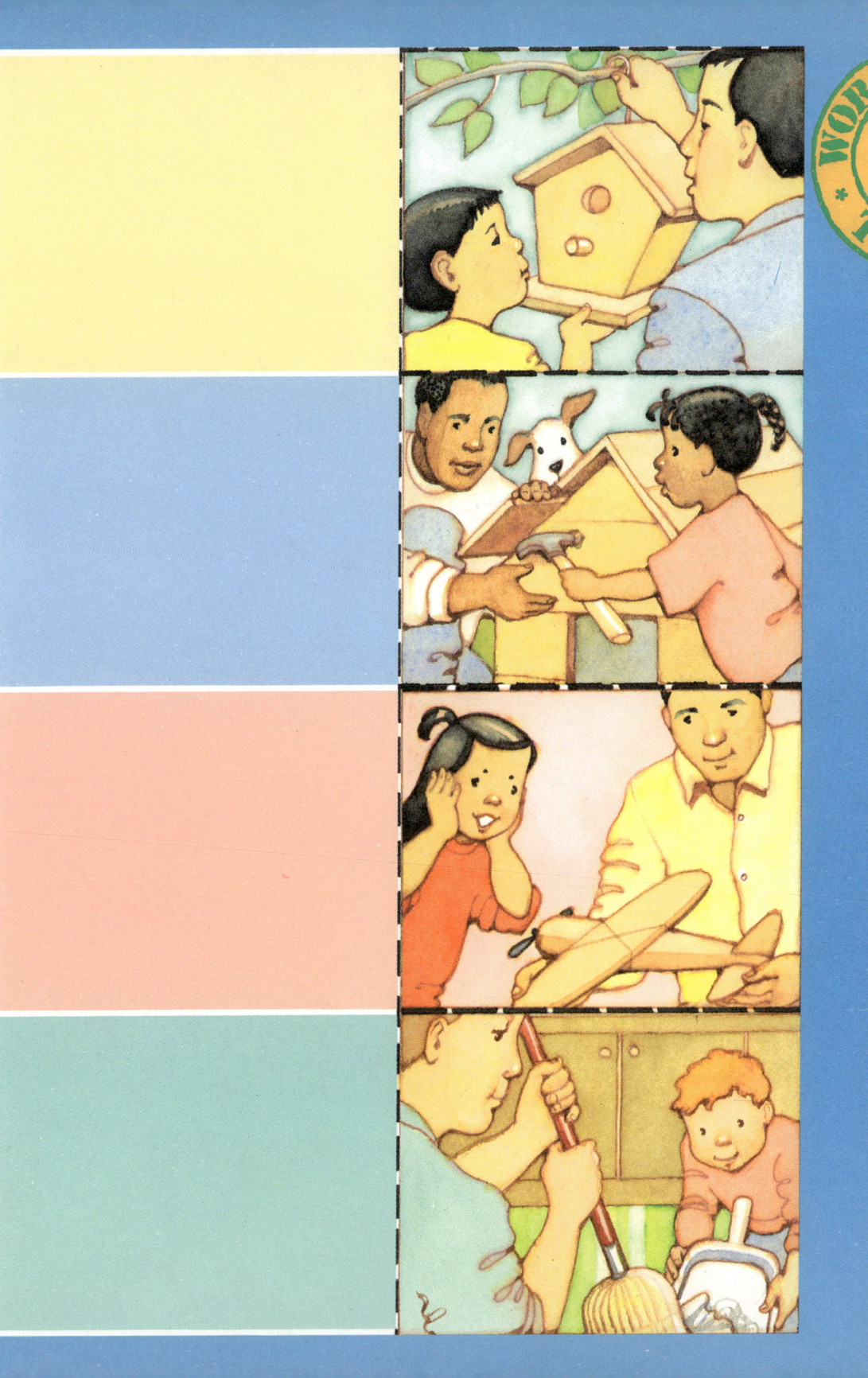

Sophie and Jack Help Out

Phonics

Children use what they have learned about compound words to help them read the sentences. Then they decide which picture goes with each sentence, cut out the pictures, and paste them next to matching text.

Sophie and Jack Help Out

Responding

Using sentence patterns from the story, children write about other jobs Sophie and Jack might do together to help their Papa. Then children illustrate their work and share it with others.

_____
_____
"I'll _____," said Sophie.
"I'll help," said Jack.
_____
_____
"I'll _____," said Jack.
"I'll help," said Sophie.

91

Sophie and Jack Help Out
Phonics

Children finish sentences, using the words listed, that tell about more things Sophie and Jack do in the spring. Then children may read the completed sentences aloud.

Sophie and Jack fix the _____.

They play with a _____.

They draw a special _____.

They have fun with Sophie's _____.

They jump into the _____.

They hide in a _____.

map
lake
hat
cave
bat
gate

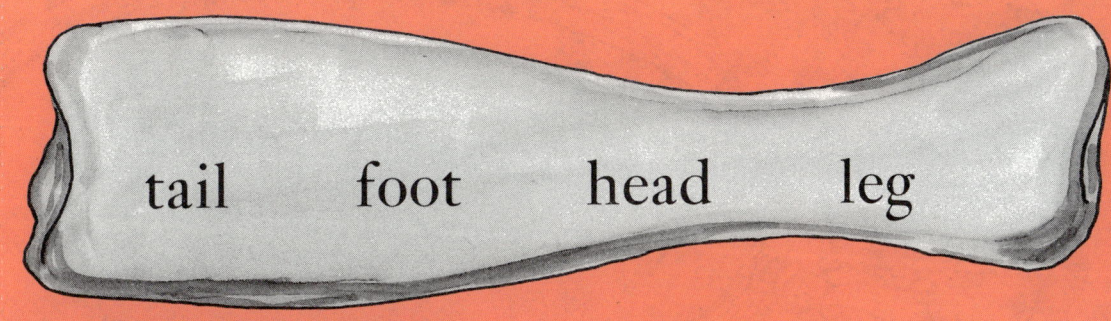

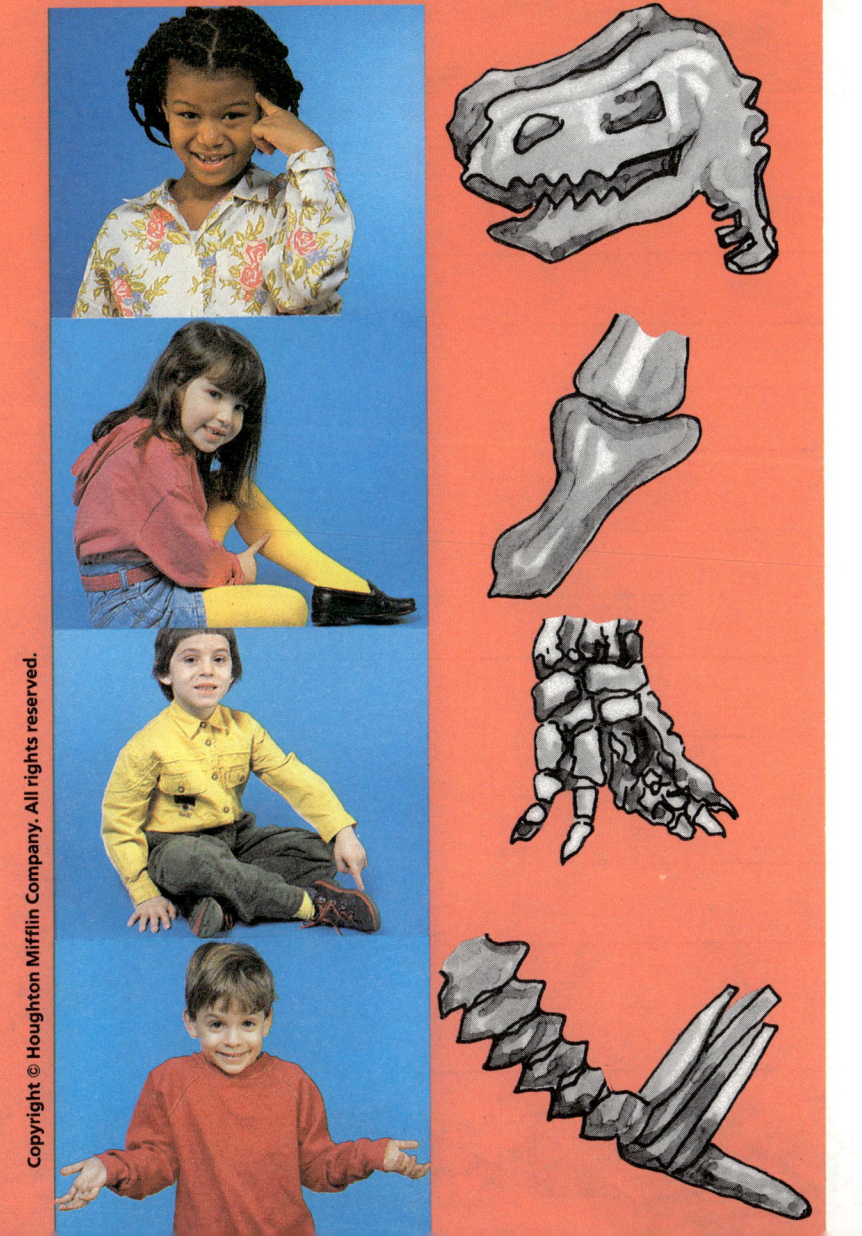

tail   foot   head   leg

Dinosaurs had _____ bones.
So do you.

Dinosaurs had _____ bones.
So do you.

Dinosaurs had _____ bones.
So do you.

Dinosaurs had _____ bones.
Do YOU?

Bones, Bones, Dinosaur Bones
Decoding
Children read each sentence pair and look at the picture. They use what they have learned about decoding to read the words at the top and choose an appropriate word to write in the lines. Children may then draw and label pictures of other dinosaur bones.

93

Bones, Bones, Dinosaur Bones
Vocabulary

In this activity, children print each word from the box next to the related phrase. Children may choose to illustrate the items.

Words. Words. We look for words.

| garden   house   early   bread |

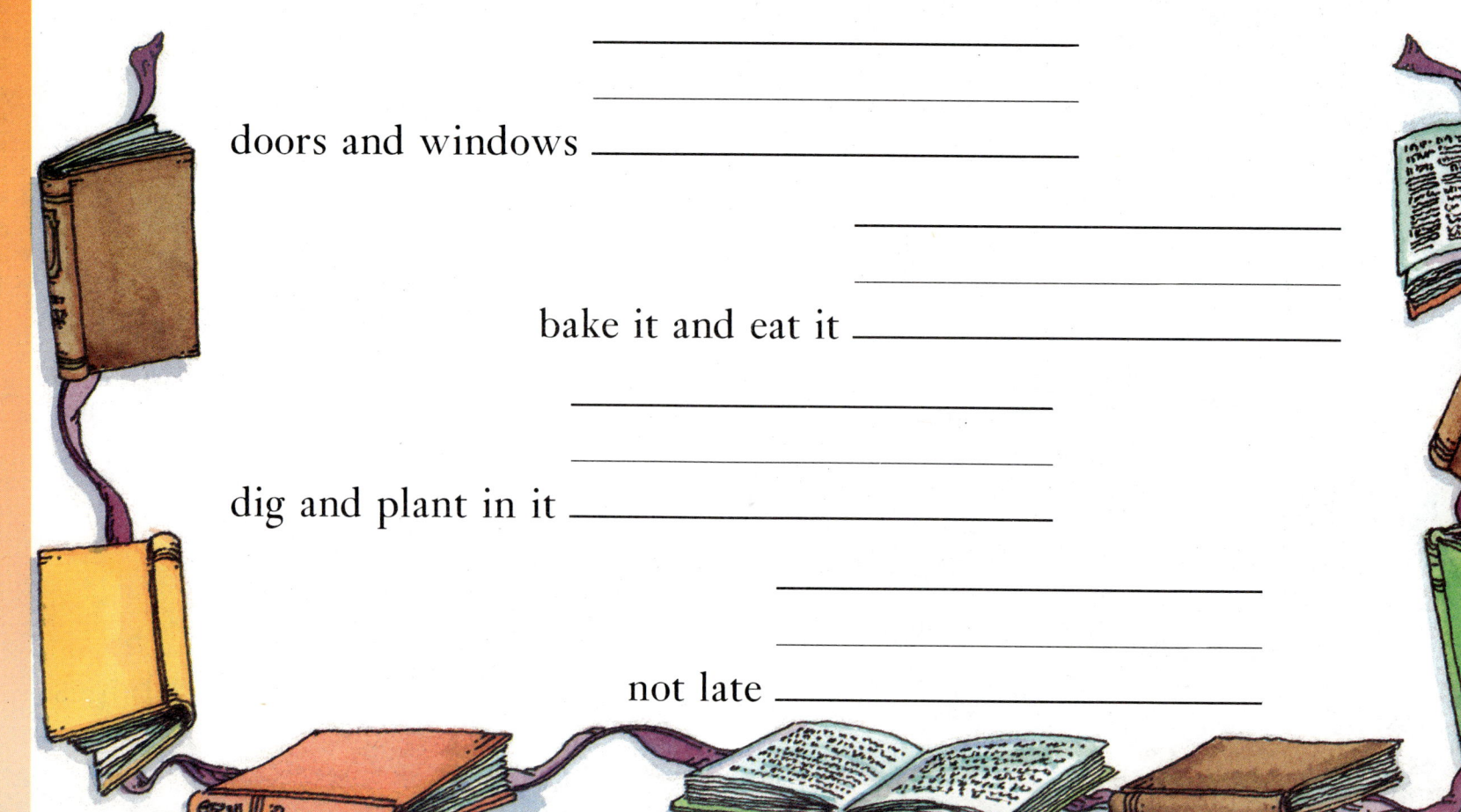

doors and windows _____

bake it and eat it _____

dig and plant in it _____

not late _____

Something Special

by _____

Introducing the Theme

Responding

Children draw a picture of the special thing they are most looking forward to reading about. Then they write their names in the space provided.

The Writing Center

Beginning

A Special Toy

The Writing Center

After talking about toys and special toys, children draw the beginning of a story about a special toy. Then they write or tell about the pictures they drew.

Middle

A *Special Toy*

The Writing Center

Children draw their ideas for the middle of their story about a special toy. Then they write or tell about the pictures.

A Special Toy

The Writing Center

Children draw their ideas for the end of their story about a special toy. Then they write or tell about the pictures they drew.

End

98

A Special Toy

A Special Toy
The Writing Center
Children review the beginning, the middle, and the end of their story. Then they draw and write or tell their completed story. Finally, they share their story with friends or family.

99

My Brown Bear Barney

Responding

Children respond to these questions: Do you think the girl in the story does some fun, special things? Which thing would you most like to do? Children draw and caption pictures of themselves doing one of those special things.

When I go _____,
I take...

and my brown bear Barney.

Something Special

My Brown Bear Barney **Responding**

Children think of another place the girl in the story *My Brown Bear Barney* might go. They draw pictures of the things she might take with her and label each item.

Something Special

My Brown Bear Barney
Decoding

Children read the sentences at the top. Then they read each story title and look at the picture. They choose a word from the list that rhymes with the word in heavy, dark letters, and print it in the lines to complete the title. Children may want to choose one of the titles and make up their own story to go with it.

102

I made up some special stories. Help me name them.

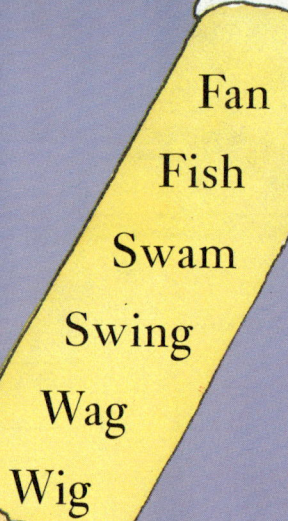

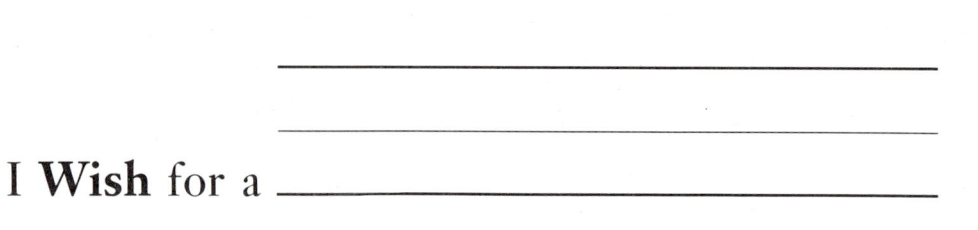

Fan
Fish
Swam
Swing
Wag
Wig

The **Pig** with a _____

I **Wish** for a _____

I **Sing** in the _____

Special Words

My Brown Bear Barney
Responding

Children make a list of words from *My Brown Bear Barney* that they liked and might want to use in their own writing.

Something Special

If I Had a Pig
Responding

Ask: How do you think the boy felt about animals, even though his pig wasn't real? Children draw a real pet they think the boy would like. Then they give the boy a name and write that name in the caption.

A pet for _____

104

rice ride
kite bike

If I had a _____,
I would fly it.

If I had some _____,
I would eat it.

If I had a _____,
I would _____ it.

If I Had a Pig
Phonics

Children complete each sentence, using the pictures as clues and choosing from the listed words. Then children may read their completed sentences aloud.

105

If I Had a Pig
Responding

Using a sentence pattern from the story, children think of something else they might do if they had a pig. Children draw a picture and complete the pattern by dictating or writing their own stories. Children may then read their stories aloud.

If I had a pig, I would _____

Story Starter

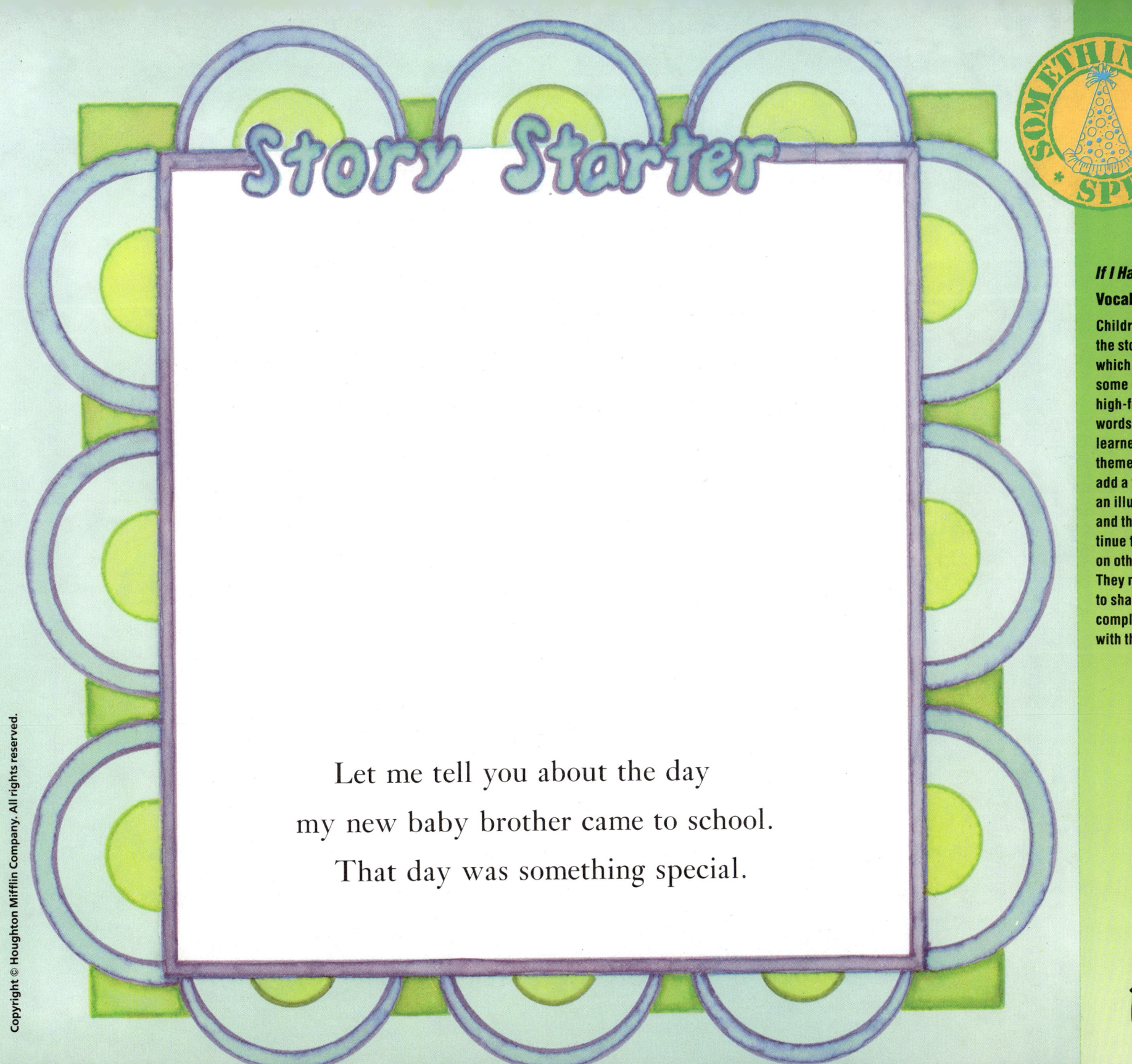

Let me tell you about the day
my new baby brother came to school.
That day was something special.

If I Had a Pig
Vocabulary
Children read the story starter, which contains some of the high-frequency words they have learned in this theme. They add a title and an illustration and then continue the story on other paper. They may choose to share their completed stories with the class.

SOMETHING SPECIAL

I Need a Lunch Box

Responding

Children recall the special lunch boxes that the boy in the story saw and dreamed about. Then they decorate the lunch box on this page to show how *they* would make it special. Some children may also want to design new features such as wheels, a combination lock, or a window for viewing what's inside. Children may write about their lunch boxes on another sheet of paper.

108

Copyright © Houghton Mifflin Company. All rights reserved.

Thanks, Mommy and Daddy! _____

I **didn't** have a lunch box. _____

That's what I wished for. _____

You've made me so happy. _____

I'll take it everywhere! _____

I Need a Lunch Box
Decoding
Using what they have learned about contractions, children read some sentences that the boy might have said when he got a new lunch box. In the lines after each sentence, they write the two words that the contraction stands for.

I Need a Lunch Box

Responding

Children think of things *they* could carry in a lunch box each day of the week, such as food items, small games or toys, messages, or pencils. Then they complete the sentence pattern from the story by writing words to tell what they might carry each day. Some children may want to add a small picture of the item next to each phrase.

_____
_____ for Monday…

_____
_____ for Tuesday…

_____
_____ for Wednesday…

_____
_____ for Thursday…

_____
_____ for Friday.

110

If I had a lunch box, I could keep my cards in it!

SOMETHING SPECIAL

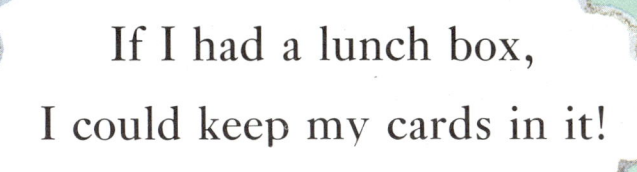

five

fine

fish

one

thin

pine

six

white

mice

a

nice

big

kite

I Need a Lunch Box
Phonics

Children cut out the cards. Then they use what they have learned about long and short *i* sounds to help them read each phrase and match it with the right picture. They paste the two cards together back to back. Children may want to make other picture cards for classmates to match, with such phrases as *five big ships, a pile of rice,* and *six thick bricks.*

111

| catch | watched | ready | breakfast |

Roberto, Daniel, and Papa had **something to eat.** _____

Then they were **all set** to go fishing. _____

Roberto and Papa didn't **get** a fish… _____

…but Daniel did!
Then everyone **looked at** Daniel! _____

Daniel Goes Fishing
Decoding
Children read each sentence. Then they choose a word from the list that means about the same as the word(s) in heavy, dark letters and write it in the lines. Children may want to read the sentences aloud, substituting the words they wrote for the boldfaced ones.

What's It About?

SOMETHING SPECIAL

Daniel Goes Fishing

Vocabulary

Children read each sentence, decide what special thing a story with that title might be about, and choose a word to complete the sentence. They may want to write a story of their own based on one of the titles.

glasses   prize   bike

"Zooming on Two Wheels" could be _____
_____
about a _____ race.

"Now I Can See Much More!" could be about
_____
_____
someone who gets new _____.

"The Best Dinosaur Drawing" could be about
_____
_____
a picture that wins a _____.

114

Reading on My Own

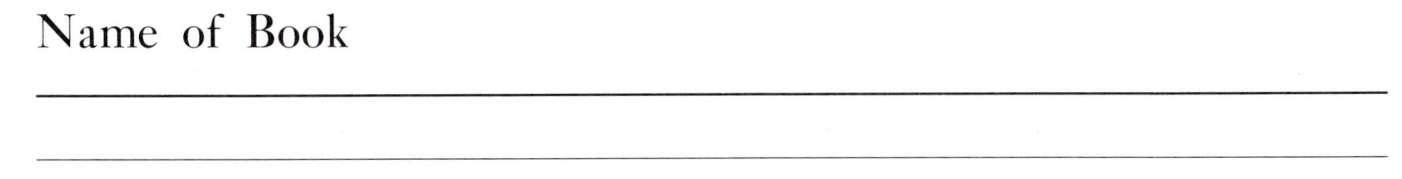

Name of Book
_____
_____

Name of Book
_____
_____

Name of Book
_____
_____

Name of Book
_____
_____

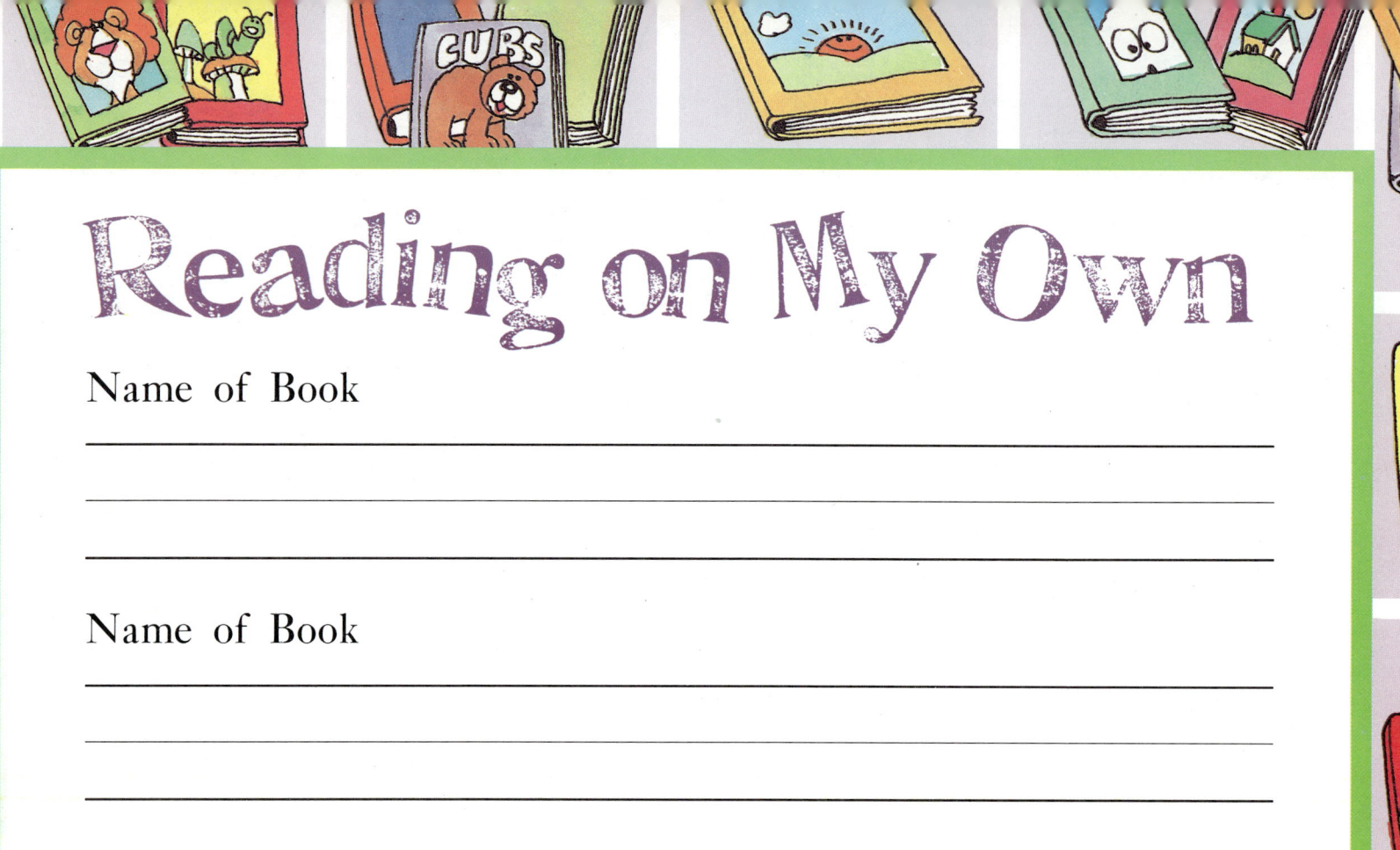

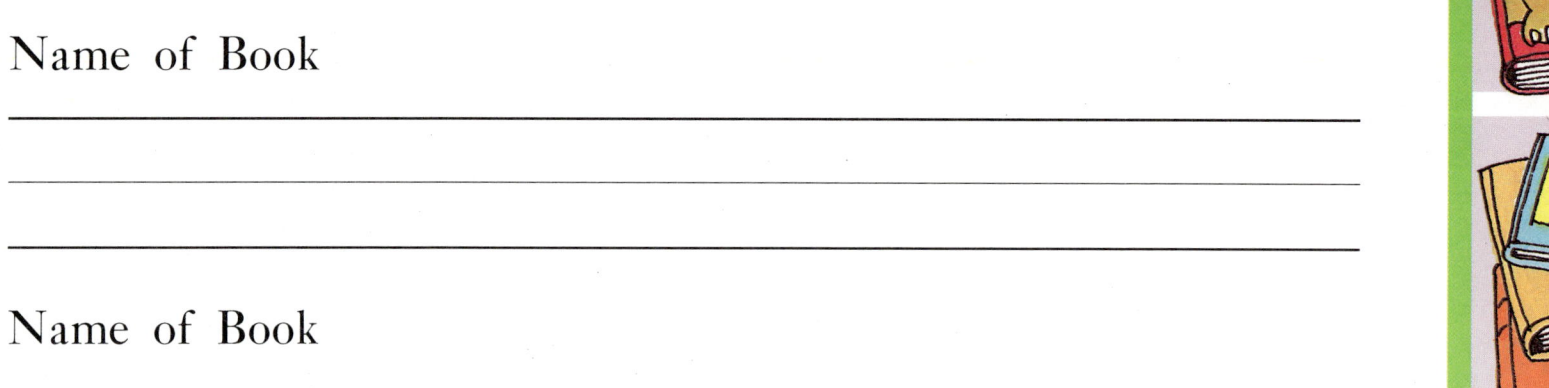

Reading on My Own

Name of Book
_____
_____
_____

Name of Book
_____
_____
_____

Name of Book
_____
_____
_____

Name of Book
_____
_____
_____

Reading on My Own

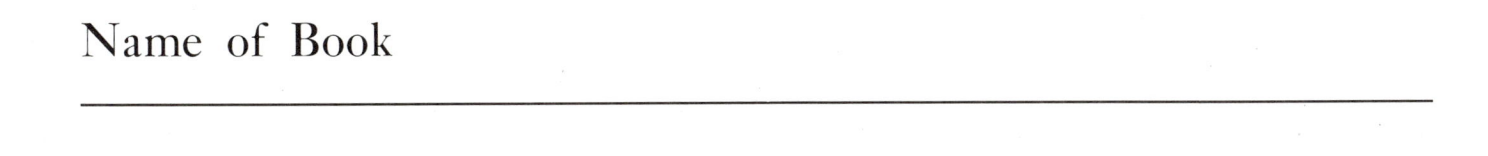

Name of Book
_____
_____

Name of Book
_____
_____

Name of Book
_____
_____

Name of Book
_____
_____

Reading on My Own

Name of Book
_____
_____
_____

Name of Book
_____
_____
_____

Name of Book
_____
_____
_____

Name of Book
_____
_____
_____

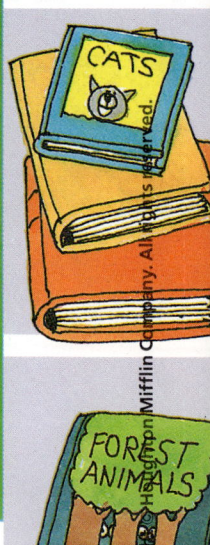

THE SPELLING GUIDE

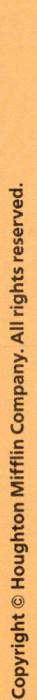

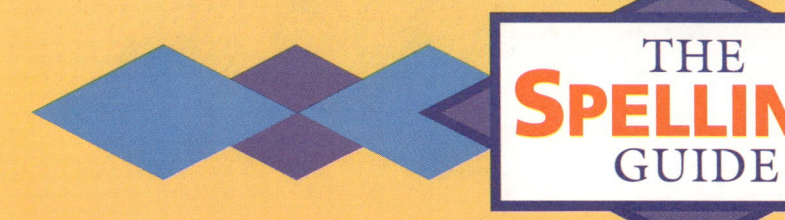

How to Study a Word

1 LOOK at the word. Name each letter.

2 SAY the word.

3 THINK about the word.

4 WRITE the word.

5 CHECK the spelling.

119

SPELLING LIST

Sophie and Jack Help Out

The Long a Sound
rake   came   late

Spelling Words
1. rake
2. came
3. make
4. name
5. take
6. late

Challenge Words
1. place
2. shade

Your Own Words
Add your own spelling words on the back. →

SPELLING LIST

Raking Leaves

The Short a Sound
ran   am   cat

Spelling Words
1. ran
2. am
3. cat
4. bag
5. hat
6. man

Challenge Words
1. grass
2. ask

Your Own Words
Add your own spelling words on the back. →

SPELLING LIST

Potluck

Words with at, ad, or an
at   had   an
sat   bad   can

Spelling Words
1. at
2. had
3. sat
4. an
5. bad
6. can

Challenge Words
1. that
2. glad

Your Own Words
Add your own spelling words on the back. →

SPELLING AND WRITING WORD LISTS

Your Own Words

1. _____
2. _____
3. _____
4. _____

Writer's Words from the Story

Learn to spell these words to use in your own writing.
1. the
2. and
3. a

SPELLING AND WRITING WORD LISTS

Your Own Words

1. _____
2. _____
3. _____
4. _____

Writer's Words from the Story

Learn to spell these words to use in your own writing.
1. to
2. I
3. for

SPELLING AND WRITING WORD LISTS

Your Own Words

1. _____
2. _____
3. _____
4. _____

Writer's Words from the Story

Learn to spell these words to use in your own writing.
1. was
2. you
3. they

SPELLING LIST

I Need a Lunch Box

The Long i Sound

five like mine

Spelling Words

1. five
2. like
3. mine
4. time
5. hide
6. bike

Challenge Words

1. twice
2. write

Your Own Words

Add your own spelling words on the back. ⇢

123

SPELLING LIST

If I Had a Pig

The Short i Sound

it if him

Spelling Words

1. it
2. if
3. him
4. pig
5. did
6. hit

Challenge Words

1. with
2. milk

Your Own Words

Add your own spelling words on the back. ⇢

123

SPELLING LIST

My Brown Bear Barney

Words with in, ig, or ix

in big six
win dig fix

Spelling Words

1. in
2. big
3. six
4. dig
5. fix
6. win

Challenge Words

1. thin
2. chin

Your Own Words

Add your own spelling words on the back. ⇢

123

SPELLING AND WRITING WORD LISTS

Your Own Words

1. _____
2. _____
3. _____
4. _____

Writer's Words from the Story

Learn to spell these words to use in your own writing.

1. when
2. from
3. some

SPELLING AND WRITING WORD LISTS

Your Own Words

1. _____
2. _____
3. _____
4. _____

Writer's Words from the Story

Learn to spell these words to use in your own writing.

1. of
2. have
3. his

SPELLING AND WRITING WORD LISTS

Your Own Words

1. _____
2. _____
3. _____
4. _____

Writer's Words from the Story

Learn to spell these words to use in your own writing.

1. one
2. all
3. said